Tinker Bell

Two Magical Tales

Tinker Bell

Two Magical Tales

THE TROUBLE WITH TINK
AND
TINK, NORTH OF NEVER LAND

A STEPPING STONE BOOK™
RANDOM HOUSE 🏠 NEW YORK

ISBN: 978-0-7364-2589-6
www.randomhouse.com/kids/disney
Printed in the United States of America
10 9 8 7 6 5 4 3 2 1

All About Fairies

IF YOU HEAD toward the second star on your right and fly straight on till morning, you'll come to Never Land, a magical island where mermaids play and children never grow up.

When you arrive, you might hear something like the tinkling of little bells. Follow that sound and you'll find Pixie Hollow, the secret heart of Never Land.

A great old maple tree grows in Pixie Hollow, and in it live hundreds of fairies and sparrow men. Some of them can do water magic, others can fly like the wind, and still others can speak to animals. You see, Pixie Hollow is the Never fairies' kingdom, and each fairy who lives there has a special, extraordinary talent.

Not far from the Home Tree, nestled in the branches of a hawthorn, is Mother Dove, the most magical creature of all. She sits on her egg, watching over the fairies, who in turn watch over her. For as long as Mother Dove's egg stays well and whole, no one in Never Land will ever grow old.

Once, Mother Dove's egg *was* broken. But we are not telling the story of the egg here. Now it is time for Tinker Bell's tale. . . .

Disney fairies

The
Trouble
with
Tink

The Trouble with Tink

WRITTEN BY
KIKI THORPE

ILLUSTRATED BY
JUDITH HOLMES CLARKE
& THE DISNEY STORYBOOK ARTISTS

A STEPPING STONE BOOK™
RANDOM HOUSE 🏠 NEW YORK

ONE SUNNY, BREEZY afternoon in Pixie Hollow, Tinker Bell sat in her workshop, frowning at a copper pot. With one hand, she clutched her tinker's hammer, and with the other, she tugged at her blond bangs, which was Tink's habit when she was thinking hard about something. The pot had been squashed nearly flat on one side. Tink was trying to determine how to tap it to make it right again.

All around Tink lay her tinkering tools: baskets full of rivets, scraps of tin, pliers, iron wire, and swatches of steel wool for scouring a pot until it shone. On the walls hung portraits of some of the pans and ladles and washtubs Tink had mended. Tough jobs were always Tink's favorites.

Tink was a pots-and-pans fairy, and her greatest joy came from fixing things. She loved anything metal that could be cracked or dented. Even her workshop was made from a teakettle that had once belonged to a Clumsy.

Ping! Ping! Ping! Tink began to pound away. Beneath Tink's hammer the copper moved as easily as if she were smoothing the folds in a blanket.

Tink had almost finished when a shadow fell across her worktable. She looked up and saw a dark figure silhouetted in the sunny doorway. The edges of the silhouette sparkled.

"Oh, hi, Terence. Come in," said Tink.

Terence moved out of the sunlight and into the room, but he continued to shimmer. Terence was a dust-talent sparrow man. He measured and handed out the fairy dust that allowed Never Land's fairies to fly and do their magic. As a result, he was dustier than most fairies, and he sparkled all the time.

"Hi, Tink. Are you working? I mean, I see you're working. Are you almost done? That's a nice pot," Terence said, all in a rush.

"It's Violet's pot. They're dyeing spider silk tomorrow, and she needs it for boiling the dye," Tink replied. She looked eagerly at Terence's hands and sighed when she saw that they were empty. Terence stopped by Tink's workshop nearly every day. Often he brought a broken pan or a mangled sieve for her to fix. Other times, like now, he just brought himself.

"That's right, tomorrow is dyeing day," said Terence. "I saw the harvest talents bringing in the blueberries for the dye earlier. They've got a good crop this year, they should get a nice deep blue color . . ."

As Terence rambled on, Tink looked longingly at the copper pot. She picked up her hammer, then reluctantly put it back down. *It would be rude to start tapping right now,* she thought. Tink liked talking to Terence. But she liked tinkering more.

"Anyway, Tink, I just wanted to let you

know that they're starting a game of tag in the meadow. I thought maybe you'd like to join in," Terence finished.

Tink's wing tips quivered. It had been ages since there had been a game of fairy tag. Suddenly, she felt herself bursting with the desire to play, the way you fill up with a sneeze just before it explodes.

She glanced down at the pot again. The dent was nearly smooth. Tink thought she could easily play a game of tag and still have time to finish her work before dinner.

Standing up, she slipped her tinker's hammer into a loop on her belt and smiled at Terence.

"Let's go," she said.

When Tink and Terence got to the meadow, the game of tag was already in full swing. Everywhere spots of bright color wove in and out of the tall grass as fairies darted after each other.

Fairy tag is different from the sort of tag that humans, or Clumsies, as the fairies call them, play. For one thing, the fairies fly rather than run. For another, the fairies don't just chase each other until one is tagged "it." If that were the case, the fast-flying-talent fairies would win every time.

In fairy tag, the fairies and sparrow men all use their talents to try to win. And when a fairy is tagged, by being tapped on her head and told "Choose you," that fairy's whole talent group—or at least all those who are playing—becomes "chosen."

Games of fairy tag are large, complicated, and very exciting.

As Tink and Terence joined the game, a huge drop of water came hurtling through the air at them. Terence ducked, and the drop splashed against a dandelion behind him. The water-talent fairies were "chosen," Tink realized.

As they sped through the tall grass, the water fairies hurled balls of water at the other fairies. When the balls hit, they burst like water balloons and dampened the fairies' wings. This slowed them down, which helped the water fairies gain on them.

Already the other talents had organized their defense. The animal-talent fairies, led by Beck and Fawn, had rounded up a crew of chipmunks to ride when their wings got too wet to fly. The light-talent fairies bent the sunshine as they flew through it, so rays of light always shone in the eyes of the fairies chasing them. Tink saw that the pots-and-pans fairies had used washtubs to create makeshift catapults. They were trying to catch the balls of water and fling them back at the water fairies.

As Tink zipped down to join them, she heard a voice above her call, "Watch out, Tinker Bell! I'll choose you!" She looked up. Her friend Rani, a water-talent fairy, was circling above her on the back of a dove. Rani was the only fairy in the kingdom who didn't have wings. She'd cut hers off to help save Never Land when Mother Dove's egg had been destroyed. Now Brother Dove did her flying for her.

Rani lifted her arm and hurled a water

ball. It wobbled through the air and splashed harmlessly on the ground, inches away from Tink. Tink laughed, and so did Rani.

"I'm such a terrible shot!" Rani cried happily.

Just then, the pots-and-pans fairies fired a catapult. The water flew at Rani and drenched her. Rani laughed even harder.

"Choose you!"

The shout rang through the meadow. All the fairies stopped midflight and turned. A water-talent fairy named Tally was standing over Jerome, a dust-talent sparrow man. Her hand was on his head.

"Dust talent!" Jerome sang out.

Abruptly, the fairies rearranged themselves. Anyone who happened to be near a dust-talent fairy immediately darted away. The other fairies hovered in the air, waiting to see what the dust talents would do.

Tink caught sight of Terence near a tree stump a few feet away. Terence grinned at her. She coyly smiled back—and then she bolted. In a flash, Terence was after her.

Tink dove into an azalea bush. Terence was right on her heels. Tink's sides ached with laughter, but she kept flying. She wove in and out of the bush's branches. She made a hairpin turn around a thick branch. Then she dashed toward an opening in the leaves and headed back to the open meadow.

But suddenly, the twigs in front of her closed like a gate. Tink skidded to a stop and watched as the twigs wrapped around themselves. With a flick of fairy dust, Terence had closed the branches of the bush. It was the simplest magic. But Tink was trapped.

She turned as Terence flew up to her.

"Choose you," he said, placing his hand on her head. But he said it softly. None of the rest of the fairies could have heard.

Just then, a shout rang out across the meadow: "Hawk!"

At once, Tink and Terence dropped down under the azalea bush's branches. Through the leaves, Tink could see the other fairies ducking for cover. The scout who had spotted the hawk hid in the branches of a nearby elm tree. The entire meadow seemed to hold its breath as the hawk's shadow moved across it.

When it was gone, the fairies waited a few moments, then slowly came out of their hiding places. But the mood had changed. The game of tag was over.

Tink and Terence climbed out of the bush.

"I must finish Violet's pot before dinner," Tink told Terence. "Thank you for telling me about the game."

"I'm really glad you came, Tink," said Terence. He gave her a sparkling smile, but Tink didn't see it. She was already flying away, thinking about the copper pot.

Tink's fingers itched to begin working again. As she neared her workshop, she reached for her tinker's hammer hanging on her belt. Her fingertips touched the leather loop.

Tink stopped flying. Frantically, she ran her fingers over the belt loop again and again. Her hammer was gone.

2

TINK SKIMMED OVER the ground, back the way she'd come. Her eyes darted this way and that. She was hoping to catch a glimmer of metal in the tall grass.

"Fool," Tink told herself. "You foolish, foolish fairy."

When she reached the meadow, her heart sank. The trees on the far side of the meadow cast long shadows across the ground. To Tink, the meadow looked huge, like a vast jungle of waving grass and wild-flowers. How would she ever find her hammer in there?

Just then, her eyes fell on the azalea bush. *Of course!* Tink thought. *I must have dropped it when I was dodging Terence.*

Tink flew to the bush. She checked the ground beneath it and checked each branch. She paid particular attention to the places where a pots-and-pans fairy's hammer might get caught. Then she checked them again. And again. But the hammer was nowhere in sight.

Fighting back tears, Tink flew across the open meadow. She tried to recall her zigzagging path in the tag game. Eventually she gave that up and began to search the meadow inch by inch, flying close to the ground. She parted the petals of wildflowers. She peered into rabbit burrows. She looked everywhere she could think of, even places she knew the hammer couldn't possibly be.

As Tink searched, the sun sank into a red pool on the horizon, then disappeared. A thin sliver of moon rose in the sky. The night was so dark that even if Tink had flown over the hammer, she wouldn't have been able to see it. But the hammer was already long gone. A Never crow had spotted it hours before and, attracted by its shine, had carried it off to its nest.

The grass was heavy with dew by the time Tink slowly started back to the Home Tree. As she flew, tears of frustration rolled down her cheeks. She swiped them away. *What will I do without my hammer?* Tink wondered. It was her most important tool. She thought of the copper pot waiting patiently for her in her workshop, and more tears sprang to her eyes.

It might seem that it should have been easy for Tink to get another tinker's hammer, but in fact, it was not. In the fairy kingdom, there is just the right amount of everything; no more, no less. A tool-making fairy would need Never iron to make a new hammer. And a mining-talent fairy would have to collect the iron. Because their work was difficult, the mining-talent fairies only mined once in a moon cycle, when the moon was full. Tink eyed the thin silver slice in the sky. Judging from the moon, that wouldn't be for many days.

For a pots-and-pans fairy, going many days without fixing pots or pans would be like not eating or sleeping. To Tink, the idea was horrible.

But that wasn't the only reason she

was crying. Tink had a secret. She *did* have a spare hammer. But it was at Peter Pan's hideout—she had accidentally left it there quite a while before. And she was terribly scared about going back to get it.

Tink got back to the Home Tree, but she was too upset to go inside and sleep. Instead, she flew up to the highest branch and perched there. She looked up at the stars and tried to figure out what to do.

Tink thought about Peter Pan: his wild red hair, his freckled nose turned up just so, his eyes that looked so happy when he laughed. She remembered the time that she and Peter had gone to the beach to skip rocks on the lagoon. One of the rocks had accidentally nicked a mermaid's tail as she dove beneath the water. The mermaid had

scolded them so ferociously that Peter and Tink had fled laughing all the way to the other side of the island.

Tink's heart ached. Remembering Peter Pan was something she almost never let herself do. Since he had brought the Wendy to Never Land, Tink and Peter had hardly spoken.

No, Tink decided. She couldn't go to Peter's for the spare hammer. It would make her too sad.

"I'll make do without it," she told herself. What was a hammer, after all, but just another tool?

3

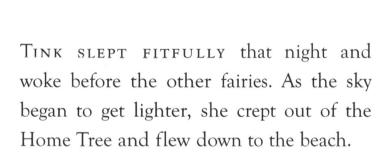

TINK SLEPT FITFULLY that night and woke before the other fairies. As the sky began to get lighter, she crept out of the Home Tree and flew down to the beach.

In one corner of the lagoon, there was a small cave that could only be entered at low tide. Tink flew in and landed on the damp ground. The floor of the cave was covered with sea-polished pebbles. This was

where Peter had come to get stones for skipping on the water, Tink remembered.

Tink carefully picked her way through
the rocks. Many of them were as big as her
head. They were all smooth and shiny with
seawater.

At last Tink picked up a reddish pebble the size and shape of a sunflower seed. She hefted it once into the air and caught it again.

"This might work," Tink said aloud into the empty cave.

Might work, her voice echoed back to her.

As the tide rose and the waves began to roll in, Tink flew out of the cave, gripping the pebble in her fist.

Back in her workshop, Tink used iron wire to bind the flat side of the rock to a twig. With a pinch of fairy dust, she tightened the wires so the rock was snug against the wood. She held up her makeshift hammer and looked at it.

"It's not so bad," she said. She tried to sound positive.

Taking a deep breath, Tink began to tap the copper pot.

Clank! Clank! Clank! Tink winced as the horrible sound echoed through her workshop. With each blow, the copper pot seemed to shudder.

"I'm sorry, I'm sorry!" Tink whispered to the pot. She tried to tap more gently.

The work took forever. Each strike with the pebble hammer left a tiny dent. Slowly, the bent copper straightened out. But the pot's smooth, shiny surface was now as pitted and pockmarked as the skin of a grapefruit.

Tink fought back tears. *It's no good*, she thought. *This pebble doesn't work at all!*

Tink raised her arm to give the pot one last tap. Just then, the pebble flew off the stick and landed with a clatter in a pile of tin scrap, as if to say it agreed.

Suddenly, the door of Tink's workshop burst open and a fairy flew in. She wore a gauzy dress tie-dyed in a fancy pattern of blues and greens. Her cheeks were bright splotches of pink. Corkscrews of curly red hair stood out in all directions from her head, and her hands were stained purple with berry juice. She looked as if she had been painted using all the colors in a watercolor box. It was Violet, the pot's owner, a dyeing-talent fairy.

"Tink! Thank goodness you're almost done with the . . . Oh!" Violet exclaimed. She stopped and stared. Tink was standing over the copper pot, gripping a twig as if she planned to beat it like a drum.

"Oh, Violet, hi. Yes, I'm, er . . . I'm done with the pot. That is, mostly," Tink said. She put down the twig. With the other hand, she tugged nervously at her bangs.

"It looks . . . uh . . ." Violet's voice trailed off as she eyed the battered pot. Tink was the best pots-and-pans fairy in the kingdom. Violet didn't want to sound as if she was criticizing her work.

"It needs a couple of touch-ups, but I fixed the squashed part," Tink reassured her. "It's perfectly good for boiling dye in. We can try it now if you like."

The door of Tink's workshop opened again. Terence came in, carrying a ladle that was so twisted it looked as if it had been tied in a knot.

"Hi, Tink! I brought you a ladle to fix!" he called out. "Oh, hello, Violet! Dropping off?" he asked as he spied the copper pot.

"No . . . er, picking up," Violet said worriedly.

"Oh," said Terence. He looked back at the pot in surprise.

Tink filled a bucket with water from a rain barrel outside her workshop and brought it over to her worktable. As Violet and Terence watched, she poured the water into the copper pot.

"See?" Tink said to Violet. "It's good as—"

Just then, they heard a metallic creaking sound. Suddenly—*plink, plink, plink,*

plink! One by one, tiny streams of water burst through the damaged copper. The pot looked more like a watering can than something to boil dye in.

"Oh!" Violet and Terence gasped. They turned to Tink, their eyes wide.

Tink felt herself blush, but she couldn't tear her eyes away from the leaking pot. She had never failed to fix a pot before, much less made it worse than it was when she got it.

The thing was, no fairy ever failed at her talent. To do so would mean you weren't really talented at all.

After a long, awkward silence, Violet closed her mouth, cleared her throat, and said, "I can probably share a dye pot with someone else. I'll come back and get this later." With a last confused glance at Tink, she hurried out the door.

Terence was also confused, but he was in no hurry to leave. He set the twisted ladle down on Tink's workbench.

"Tink, you look tired," he said gently.

"I'm not tired," said Tink.

"Maybe you need to take a break," Terence suggested. But he wasn't at all sure what Tink needed. "Why don't we fly to the tearoom? On my way here, I smelled pumpkin muffins baking in the kitchen. They smelled deli—"

"I'm not hungry," Tink interrupted, although she was starving. She hadn't had breakfast, or dinner the night before. But the talents always sat together in the tearoom. Tink didn't feel like sitting at a table with the other pots-and-pans fairies right now.

Suddenly, Tink was irritated with Terence. If he hadn't told her about the tag game, she never would have lost her hammer. Tink knew she wasn't being fair. But she was upset and embarrassed, and she wanted someone to blame.

"I can't talk today, Terence," she snapped. She turned toward a pile of baking tins that needed repair and tugged at her bangs. "I have a lot of work, and I'm already behind."

"Oh." Terence's shoulders sagged. "Just let me know if you need anything," he said, and headed for the door. "Bye, Tink."

As soon as Terence was gone, Tink flew to a nearby birch tree where a carpenter-talent sparrow man worked and asked if she could borrow his hammer. The sparrow man agreed, provided that she brought it back in two days' time. He was in the middle of cutting oak slats for some repairs in the Home Tree, he said, and wouldn't need the hammer until he was through. Tink promised she would.

Two days. Tink didn't know what she'd do after that. But she wasn't going to think about it, she decided. Not just yet.

When Tink entered her empty workshop, something seemed different. There was a sweet smell in the air. Then she spied a plate with a pumpkin muffin on it and a cup of buttermilk on her workbench.

Terence, Tink thought. She was sorry that she'd snapped at him earlier.

The muffin was moist, sweet, and still warm from the oven, and it melted on her tongue. The buttermilk was cool and tart. As soon as she'd eaten, Tink felt better.

She picked up the carpenter's hammer

and began to work on a stack of pie pans. The pans weren't cracked or dented, but Dulcie, the baking-talent fairy who'd brought them to her, complained that the pies she baked in them kept burning. Tink thought it had something to do with the pans' shape, or maybe the tin on the bottom of the pans was too thin.

The carpenter's hammer was almost twice as big as her tinker's hammer. Holding it in her hand, Tink felt as clumsy as a Clumsy.

Still, she had to admit that it was much better than the pebble.

Tink worked slowly with the awkward hammer. She reshaped the pie pans, then added an extra layer of tin to the bottom of each one. When she was done, she looked over her work.

It's not the best job I've ever done, she thought. *But it's not so bad, either.*

Tink gathered the pie pans into a stack and carried them to Dulcie. Dulcie was delighted to have them back.

"Don't miss tea this afternoon, Tink," she said with a wink as she brushed flour from her hands. "We're making strawberry pie. I'll save you an extra-big slice!"

On the way back to her workshop, Tink ran into Prilla, a young fairy with a freckled nose and a bouncy nature. Prilla always did cartwheels and handsprings when she was excited about something.

"Tink!" Prilla cried, bounding over to her. "Did you hear?"

"Hear what?" asked Tink.

"About Queen Ree's tub," Prilla told her. Ree was the fairies' nickname for their queen, Clarion. "It's sprung a leak. The queen's whole bath trickled out while she was washing this morning."

Tink's eyes widened. The bathtub was one of Queen Ree's most prized possessions. It was the size of a coconut shell and made of Never pewter, with morning glory leaves sculpted into its sides. The tub rested on four feet shaped like lions' paws, and there were two notches at the back where the queen could rest her wings to keep them dry while she took her bath.

Tink's fingers twitched. She would love to work on the bathtub.

"The queen's attendants looked all over, but they couldn't spot the leak. I thought of you when I heard, Tink," Prilla said. "Of course, Queen Ree will want you to fix it. You're the best." Prilla grinned at Tink and did a handspring.

Tink grinned back, showing her deep dimples. It was the first time she'd smiled since she lost her hammer. "I hope so, Prilla. It would be quite an honor to work on the queen's tub," she replied.

Prilla turned a one-handed cartwheel and flew on. "See you later, Tink!" she called.

Tink thought about the queen's tub all afternoon as she fixed the spout on a teakettle that wouldn't whistle. What kind of leak could it be? A hairline crack? Or a pinprick hole? Tink smiled, imagining the possibilities.

By the time Tink had finished fixing the kettle, it was nearly teatime.

"They'll need this in the kitchen," Tink said to herself as she buffed the teakettle with a piece of suede. She would take it to the kitchen, then go to the tearoom for strawberry pie. Tink's stomach rumbled hungrily at the thought. Strawberry was one of her favorite kinds of pie.

But when she got to the kitchen, a horrible smell greeted her. Tink quickly handed the teakettle to one of the cooking-talent fairies and held both hands to her nose.

"What is that smell?" she asked the fairy. "It's not strawberry pie."

But the fairy just gave her a strange look and hurried off to fill the teakettle with water.

Tink made her way through the kitchen until she found Dulcie. She was standing over several steaming pies that had just been pulled from the oven. She looked as if she might cry.

"Dulcie, what's going on?" Tink asked.

As soon as Dulcie saw Tink, her forehead wrinkled. The wrinkles made little creases in the flour on her skin, which made the lines seem even deeper.

"Oh, Tink. I don't know how to tell you this," Dulcie said. "It's the pies. They're all coming out mincemeat."

Tink turned and looked at the steaming

pies. That was where the horrible smell was coming from.

"We tried everything," Dulcie went on. "When the strawberry came out all wrong, we tried plum. When that didn't work, we tried cherry. We even tried pumpkin. But every time we pulled the pies out of the oven, they'd turned into mincemeat." Now Dulcie's chin wrinkled like a walnut as she struggled to hold back tears. Her whole face was puckered with worry.

This was indeed a kitchen disaster. Fairies hate mincemeat. To them it tastes like burned broccoli and old socks.

"Is there something wrong with the oven?" Tink asked Dulcie. She didn't know much about ovens. But if there was something metal in it, she could probably fix it.

Dulcie swallowed hard.

"No, Tink," she said. "It's the pans you fixed. Only the pies baked in those pans are the ones that get spoiled."

5

Tink's mind reeled. She took a step back from Dulcie. But before she could say anything, a shrill whistle split the air.

The tea water had boiled. A cooking-talent sparrow man hurried over to lift the kettle off the fire. Expertly, the sparrow man poured the water into the teacups until there wasn't a drop left.

But the teakettle continued to shriek.

The sparrow man lifted the kettle's lid to let out any steam that might have been caught inside. A puff of steam escaped, but the kettle still whistled on. Without pausing, it changed pitch and began to whistle a lively, earsplitting melody.

All the fairies in the kitchen, including Tink, covered their ears. Several fairies from other talents who were in the tearoom poked their heads in the door of the kitchen.

"What's all that noise?" a garden-talent fairy asked one of the baking-talent fairies.

"It's the teakettle, the one that just wouldn't whistle," the baking-talent fairy replied. She winced as the kettle hit a particularly high note. "Tink fixed it, and now it won't shut up!"

Twee-twee-tweeeeeeeeee! the teakettle shrieked cheerfully, as if confirming that what she'd said was true. The fairies cringed and clamped their hands more tightly against their ears.

"And the pie pans Tink fixed aren't any good, either," another baking-talent fairy noted over the noise. "Every pie baked in them turns into mincemeat!"

A murmur went around the room. What could this mean? the other fairies wondered. Was it some kind of bad joke? Everyone turned and looked at Tink.

Tink stared back at them, blushing so deeply her glow turned orange. Then, without thinking, she turned and fled.

Tink was sitting in the shade of a wild rosebush, deep in thought. She didn't notice Vidia, a fast-flying-talent fairy, flying overhead. Suddenly, Vidia landed right in front of Tink.

"Tinker Bell, darling," Vidia greeted her.

"Hello, Vidia," Tink replied. Of all the fairies in the kingdom, Vidia was the one

Tink liked the least. Vidia was pretty, with her long dark hair, arched eyebrows, and pouting lips. But she was selfish and mean-spirited, and at the moment she was smiling in a way Tink didn't like at all.

"I'm so *sorry* to hear about your trouble, Tink darling," Vidia said.

"It's nothing," Tink said. "I was just flustered. I'll go back to the kitchen and fix the teakettle now."

"Oh, don't worry about that. Angus was in the tearoom," Vidia said. Angus was a pots-and-pans sparrow man. "He got the teakettle to shut up. No, Tink, what I meant was, I'm sorry to hear about your *talent*."

Tink blinked. "What do you mean?"

"Oh, don't you know?" Vidia asked. "Everyone's talking about it. The rumor flying around the kingdom, Tink dear, is that you've lost your talent."

"What?" Tink leaped to her feet.

"Oh, it's such a *shame,* dearest," Vidia went on, shaking her head. "You were always such a good little tinker."

"I haven't lost my talent," Tink growled. Her cheeks were burning. Her hands were balled into fists.

"If you say so. But, sweetheart, you have to admit, your work hasn't exactly been . . . *inspired* lately. Why, even I could fix pots and pans better than that," Vidia said with a little laugh. "But I wouldn't worry too much. I'm sure they won't make you leave the fairy kingdom *forever,* even if your talent has dried up for good."

Tink looked at her coldly. *I wish you*

would leave forever, she thought. But she wasn't going to give Vidia the satisfaction of seeing that she was mad. Instead, she said, "I'm sure that would never happen, Vidia."

"Yes." Vidia gave Tink a pitying smile. "But no one really knows, do they? After all, no fairy has ever lost her talent before. But I guess we'll soon find out. You see, dear heart, I've come with a message. The queen would like to see you."

Tink's stomach did a little flip. The queen?

"She's in the gazebo," Vidia told her. "I'll let you fly there on your own. I expect you'll want to collect your thoughts. Goodbye, Tink." With a last sugary smile, Vidia flew away.

Tink's heart raced. What could this mean? Was it really possible that she could be banished from the kingdom for losing her talent?

But I haven't lost my talent! Tink thought indignantly. *I've just lost my hammer.*

With that thought in mind, Tink took a deep breath, lifted her chin, and flew off to meet the queen.

6

As she made her way to the gazebo, Tink passed a group of harvest-talent fairies filling wheelbarrows with sunflower seeds to take to the kitchen. They laughed and chatted as they worked, but as soon as they saw Tink, they all stopped talking. Silently, they watched her go by. Tink could have sworn she heard one of them whisper the word "talent."

So it's true, Tink thought. *Everyone is saying I've lost my talent.*

Tink scowled as she flew past another group of fairies who silently gawked at her. She had always hated gossip, and now she hated it even more.

The queen's gazebo sat high on a rock overlooking the fairy kingdom. Tink landed lightly on a bed of soft moss outside the entrance. All around her she heard the jingle of seashell wind chimes, which hung around the gazebo.

Inside, the gazebo was drenched in purple from the sunlight filtering through the violet petals that made up the roof. Soft, fresh fir needles carpeted the floor and gave off a piney scent.

Queen Ree stood at one of the open

windows. She was looking out at the glittering blue water of the Mermaid Lagoon, which lay in the distance beyond the fairy kingdom. When she heard Tink, she turned.

"Tinker Bell, come in," said the queen.

Tink stepped inside. She waited.

"Tink, how are you feeling?" Queen Ree asked.

"I'm fine," Tink replied.

"Are you sleeping well?" asked the queen.

"Well enough," Tink told her. *Except for last night,* she added to herself. But she didn't feel the need to tell this to the queen.

"No cough? Your glow hasn't changed color?" asked the queen.

"No," Tink replied. Suddenly, she realized that the queen was checking her for signs of fairy distemper. It was a rare illness, but very contagious. If Tink had it, she would have to be separated from the group to keep from making the whole fairy kingdom sick. "No, I'm fine," Tink repeated to reassure her. "I feel very well. Really."

When the queen heard this, she seemed to relax. It was just the slightest change in her posture, but Tink noticed, and she, too, breathed a sigh of relief. Queen Ree would not banish her, Tink realized. The queen would never make such a hasty or unfair decision. It had been mean and spiteful of Vidia to say such a thing.

"Tink, you know there are rumors...."

Queen Ree hesitated. She was reluctant to repeat them.

"They say I've lost my talent," Tink said quickly so that the queen wouldn't have to. "It's nasty gossip—and untrue. It's just that—" Tink stopped. She tugged at her bangs.

She was afraid that if she told Queen Ree about her missing hammer, the queen would think she was irresponsible.

Queen Ree waited for Tink to go on. When she didn't, the queen walked closer to her and looked into her blue eyes. "Tink," she said, "is there anything you want to tell me?"

She asked so gently that Tink felt the urge to plop down on the soft fir needles and tell her everything—about the pebble hammer and the carpenter's hammer and even about Peter Pan. But Tink had never told another fairy about Peter, and she was afraid to now.

Besides, Tink told herself, *the queen has more important things to worry about than a missing hammer.*

Tink shook her head. "No," she said. "I'm sorry my pots and pans haven't been very good lately. I'll try to do better."

Queen Ree looked carefully at her. She knew something was wrong, but she didn't know what. She only knew that Tink didn't want to tell her. "Very well," she said. As Tink turned to leave, she added, "Be good to yourself, Tink."

Outside, Tink felt better. The meeting with the queen had been nothing to worry about at all. Maybe things weren't as bad as they seemed. *All I have to do now is find a new hammer, and everything will be back to normal,* Tink thought with a burst of confidence.

"Tink!" someone called.

She looked down and saw Rani and Prilla standing knee-deep in a puddle. Tink flew down and landed at the edge.

"What are you doing?" she asked, eyeing the fairies' wet clothes and hair. She was used to seeing Rani in the water. But Prilla wasn't a water fairy.

"Rani's showing me how she makes fountains in the water," Prilla explained. "I want to learn. I thought it might be fun to try in Clumsy children's lemonade." Prilla's talent was traveling over to the mainland in the blink of an eye and visiting the children there. She was the only fairy in all of Never Land who had this talent, and it was an important one. She helped keep up children's belief in fairies, which in turn saved the fairies' lives.

Tink looked at the drenched hem of Prilla's long dress and shivered. She didn't like to get wet—it always made her feel cold. She was surprised that Prilla could stand to be in the water for so long.

"I've been trying all afternoon, but this is all I can do," Prilla told her. She took a pinch of fairy dust and sprinkled it onto the water. Then she stared hard at the spot where the dust had landed and concentrated with all her might. After a moment, a few small bubbles rose to the surface and popped.

"Like a tadpole burping," Prilla said with a sigh. "Now watch Rani."

Rani sprinkled a pinch of fairy dust on the water, then stared at the spot where it had landed. Instantly, a twelve-inch fountain of water shot up from the puddle.

Tink and Prilla clapped their hands and cheered. "If I could make just a teeny little fountain, I'd be happy," Prilla confessed to Tink. Tink nodded, though she didn't really understand. She'd never wanted to make a water fountain.

Just then, Tink heard a snuffling sound. She turned and saw that Rani was crying.

"I'm so sorry, Tink," Rani said. She pulled a damp leafkerchief from one of her many pockets and blew her nose into it. As a water fairy, Rani cried a lot and was always prepared. "About your talent, I mean."

Tink's smile faded. She tugged at her bangs. "There's nothing to be sorry about. There's nothing wrong with my talent," she said irritably.

"Don't worry, Tink," Prilla said. "I know how you feel. When I thought I didn't have a talent, it was awful." Prilla hadn't known what her talent was when she first arrived in Never Land. She'd had to figure it out on her own. "Maybe you just need to try lots of things," she advised Tink, "and then it will come to you."

"I already have a talent, Prilla," Tink said carefully.

"But maybe you need another talent, like a backup when the one you have isn't working," Prilla went on. "You could learn to make fountains with me. Rani will teach you, too, won't you, Rani?"

Rani sniffled helplessly. Tink tugged her bangs so hard that a few blond hairs came out in her fingers. What Prilla was suggesting sounded crazy to Tink. She had never wanted to do anything but fix pots and pans.

"Anyway, Tink," said Prilla, "I wouldn't worry too much about what everyone is saying about—"

"Dinner?" Rani cut Prilla off.

Prilla looked at her. "No, I meant—"

"Yes, about dinner," Rani interrupted again, more firmly. She had dried her eyes and now she was looking hard at Prilla. Rani could see that the topic of talents was upsetting Tink, and she wanted Prilla to be quiet. "It's time, isn't it?"

"Yes," said Tink. But she wasn't looking at Rani and Prilla. Her mind seemed to be somewhere else altogether.

Rani put her fingers to her mouth and whistled. They heard the sound of wings beating overhead. A moment later, Brother Dove landed on the ground next to Rani. He would take her to the tearoom.

But before Rani had even climbed onto his back, Tink took off in the direction of the Home Tree without another word. Rani and Prilla had no choice but to follow.

WHEN THEY REACHED the tearoom, Tink
said good-bye to Rani and Prilla. Rani was
going to sit with the other water-talent
fairies, and Prilla was joining her. Since
Prilla didn't have her own talent group, she
was an honorary member of many different
talents, and she sat at a different table every
night. Tonight she would sit with the water-
talent fairies and practice making fountains
in her soup.

Tink made her way over to a table under a large chandelier where the pots-and-pans fairies sat together for their meals. As she took her seat, the other fairies at the table barely looked up.

"It's a crack in the bottom, I'll bet," a fairy named Zuzu was saying. "I mended a pewter bowl once that had had boiling water poured in it when it was cold. A crack had formed right down the center." Her eyes glazed over happily as she recalled fixing the bowl.

"But don't you think it could be something around the drain, since the water leaked out so quickly?" asked Angus, the sparrow man who had fixed the whistling teakettle in the kitchen earlier that day.

A serving-talent fairy with a large soup tureen walked over to the table and began to ladle chestnut dumpling soup into the fairies' bowls. Tink noticed with pride that the ladle was one she had once repaired.

She leaned forward. "What's everyone talking about?" she asked the rest of the table.

The other fairies turned, as if noticing for the first time that Tink was sitting there.

"About Queen Ree's bathtub," Zuzu explained. "She's asked us to come fix it tomorrow. We're trying to guess what's wrong with it."

"Oh, yes!" said Tink. "I've been thinking about that, too. It might be a pinprick hole. Those are the sneakiest sorts of leaks— the water just sort of drizzles out one drop at a time." Tink laughed.

But no one joined her. She looked around the table. The other fairies were

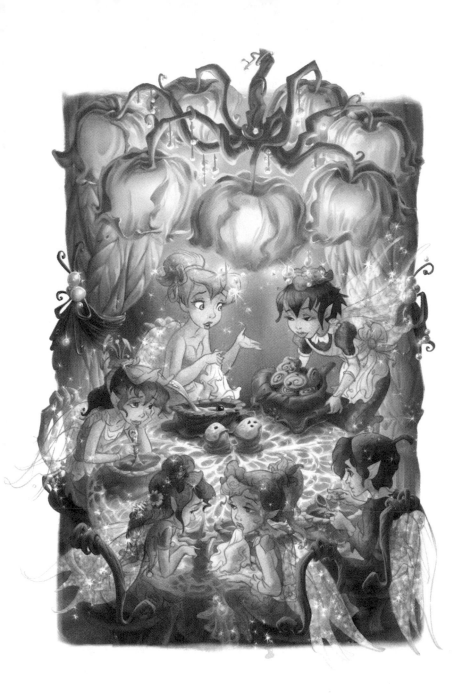

staring at her, or looking awkwardly down at their soup bowls. Suddenly, Tink realized that the queen had said nothing to her about the bathtub that afternoon in the gazebo.

"Tink," another fairy named Copper said gently, "we've all agreed that Angus and Zuzu should be the ones to repair the tub, since they are the most talented pots-and-pans fairies . . . lately, that is."

"Oh!" said Tink. "Of course." She swallowed hard. She felt as if a whole chestnut dumpling were stuck in her throat.

Now all the pots-and-pans fairies were looking at Tink with a mixture of love and concern. And, Tink was sad to see, pity.

I could just tell everyone that I lost my hammer, Tink thought. *But if they asked about the spare . . .*

Tink couldn't finish the thought. For a long, long time, Tink had neglected her pots and pans to spend all her time with Peter Pan. It was something she thought the other pots-and-pans fairies would never understand.

At last the fairies changed the topic and began to talk about the leaky pots and broken teakettles they'd fixed that day. As they chattered and laughed, Tink silently ate her soup.

Nearby, a cheer went up from the water fairies' table. Tink looked over and saw that Prilla had succeeded in making a tiny fountain in her soup.

Prilla has two talents now, Tink thought glumly. *And I haven't even got one.*

As soon as she was done with her soup, Tink put down her spoon and slipped away from the table. The other pots-and-pans fairies were so busy talking, they didn't notice her leaving.

Outside, Tink returned to the topmost branches of the Home Tree, where she'd sat the night before. She didn't want to go back to her workshop—there were pots and pans still waiting to be fixed. She didn't want to go to her room, either. It seemed too lonely there. At least here she had the stars to keep her company.

"Maybe it's true that I've lost my talent," Tink said to the stars. "If I don't have a hammer, then I can't fix things. And if I can't fix things, it's just like having no talent at all."

The stars only twinkled in reply.

From where she was sitting, Tink could see the hawthorn tree where Mother Dove lived. Between its branches, she could make out the faint shape of Mother Dove's nest. Mother Dove was the only creature in the fairy kingdom who knew all about Tink and Peter Pan. Once, after the hurricane that broke Mother Dove's wings and nearly destroyed Never Land, Tink had sat on the beach with Mother Dove and told her tales of her adventures with Peter. She had also told Mother Dove about the Wendy, and how when she came to Never Land, Peter forgot all about Tink.

What a comfort it would be to go to Mother Dove. She would know what to do.

But something held Tink back. She

remembered Mother Dove's words to her on her very first day in Never Land: *You're Tinker Bell, sound and fine as a bell. Shiny and jaunty as a new pot. Brave enough for anything, the most courageous fairy to come in a long year.* Tink had felt so proud that day.

But Tink didn't feel very brave right now, certainly not brave enough to go to Peter's and get her spare hammer. He was only a boy, but still she couldn't find the courage.

Tink couldn't bear the idea that Mother Dove would think she wasn't brave or sound or fine. It would be worse than losing her talent.

"Tink," said a voice.

Tink turned. Terence was standing behind her on the branch. She'd been so wrapped up in her thoughts, she hadn't even heard him fly up.

"I haven't fixed the ladle yet," Tink told him miserably.

"I didn't come because of the ladle," Terence replied. "I saw you leave the tearoom."

When Tink didn't explain, Terence sat down next to her on the branch. "Tink, are

you all right? Everyone is saying that . . ." He paused. Like Queen Ree, Terence couldn't bring himself to repeat the gossip. It seemed too unkind.

"That I've lost my talent," Tink finished for him. She sighed. "Maybe they're right, Terence. I can't seem to fix anything. Everything I touch comes out worse than when I started."

Terence was startled. One thing he had always admired about Tink was her fierceness: her fierce dark eyebrows, her fierce determination, even the fierce happiness of her dimpled smile. He had never seen her look as defeated as she did now.

"I don't believe that," he told her. "You're the best pots-and-pans fairy in the kingdom. Talent doesn't just go away like that."

Tink said nothing. But she felt grateful to him for not believing the rumors. For still believing in her.

"Tink," Terence asked gently, "what's really going on?"

Tink hesitated. "I lost my hammer," she blurted at last.

As soon as the words left her lips, Tink felt relieved. It was as if she'd let out a huge breath that she'd been holding in.

"Is that all it is?" Terence said. He almost laughed. It seemed like such a small thing. "But you could borrow a hammer," he suggested.

Tink told Terence about the hammer she'd made from a pebble and the one she'd borrowed from the carpenter fairy. "Neither of them works," she explained. "I need a tinker's hammer."

"Maybe there's a spare—" Terence began.

"I *have* a spare," Tink wailed. She'd already been over this so many times in her own mind. "But it's . . . I . . . I left it at Peter Pan's hideout."

"He won't give it back?" asked Terence.

Tink shook her head. "I haven't asked." She looked away.

Terence didn't know much about Peter Pan, only that Tink had been friends with him and then—suddenly—she wasn't. But he saw that Tink was upset and ashamed, and he didn't ask her anything more. Again, Tink felt a surge of gratitude toward him.

They sat silently for a moment, looking up at the stars.

"I could go with you," Terence said at last. "To Peter Pan's, I mean."

Tink's mind raced. Perhaps if someone else came along, it wouldn't be so hard to see Peter. . . .

"You would do that?" she asked.

"Tink," said Terence, "I'm your friend. You don't even need to ask."

He gave Tink a sparkling smile. This time, Tink saw it and she smiled back.

8

EARLY THE NEXT morning, before most of
the fairy kingdom was awake, Tink rapped
at the door of Terence's room. She wanted
to leave for Peter's hideout before she lost
her nerve altogether.

Terence threw open the door after the
first knock. He grinned at Tink. "Ready to
go get your talent back, Tinker Bell?"

Tink smiled. She was glad Terence was

going with her, and not just because it would be easier with someone else along.

They left Pixie Hollow just as the sun's rays shone over Torth Mountain. They flew over the banana farms, where the Tiffens were already out working in the fields. In the distance, they could hear the laughter of the mermaids in the lagoon.

"See that peak?" Tink told Terence. She pointed out a chair-shaped spot at the top of a hill. "That's called the Throne. When the Lost Boys have their skirmishes, the winner is named king of the hill. Of course, if Peter is there, he always wins. The Lost Boys wouldn't dare to beat him, even if they could," Tink explained.

"And that stream," she went on, pointing to a silver ribbon of water winding through the forest below, "leads to an underground cavern that's filled with gold and silver. Captain Hook and his men have hidden away a whole pirate ship's worth of treasure there."

Tink remembered how she had found the cavern. She had been racing along the stream in a little birchbark canoe Peter had made for her. Peter had been running along the bank. When the stream suddenly dove underground, Tink had plunged right along with it. Peter had been so thrilled with her discovery that Tink hadn't even minded the soaking she got when the canoe splashed down in the cavern.

"You must know Never Land better than any fairy in the kingdom," Terence said admiringly.

Tink looked at the island below her and felt a little twinge of pride. What Terence said was true. With Peter, Tink had explored nearly every inch of Never Land. Every rock, meadow, and hill reminded her of some adventure.

Of course, they also reminded her of Peter.

Tink felt a flutter of nervousness. How would it be to see him? What if the Wendy was there, or Peter had found someone else to play with? What if he ignored her again?

Tink fell silent. Terence, sensing that something bothered her, said nothing more for the rest of their trip.

When Tink reached the densest, darkest part of the forest, she began to glide down in a spiral. Terence followed her.

They plunged through a canopy of fig trees and landed on a white-speckled mushroom. The mushroom was nearly as wide as a Clumsy's dinner plate. Terence was surprised to feel that it was quite warm.

"It's Peter's hideout," Tink explained. "They use a mushroom cap to disguise the chimney to fool Captain Hook."

After they'd rested for a moment, Tink sprang from the mushroom and flew up to a hollow in the trunk of a nearby jackfruit tree. She was about to dive inside when Terence grabbed her wrist.

"What about owls?" he said worriedly. If there was an owl living in the hollow, it might eat them.

Tink laughed. "Anything that lived here would be terrorized by the Lost Boys. This is the entrance to the hideout!"

Peeking inside, Terence saw the entire tree was hollow, right to its roots. He followed Tink as she flew down the trunk. They came out in an underground room.

Terence looked around. The floor and walls were made of packed earth. Tree roots hung down from the ceiling, and from these, string hammocks dangled limply. Here and there on the ground lay slingshots, socks, and dirty coconut-shell bowls. The remains of a fire smoldered in a corner. The whole place had the dry, puppyish smell of little boys.

But there were no little boys in sight. The hideout was empty.

He's not home, Tink thought. She felt both disappointed and relieved.

Just then, they heard whistling coming from somewhere near the back of the den.

Tink and Terence flew toward the sound. Their glows made two bright spots of light in the dim room.

At the back of the hideout, they spied a nook that was tucked out of sight from the rest of the room. The whistling was coming from there.

When they rounded the corner, Terence saw a freckled boy with a mop of red hair sitting on a stool formed by a thick, twisted root. In one hand he held a jack-knife, and he whistled as he worked it over a piece of wood. A fishing pole leaned against the wall behind him. Looking more closely, Terence saw that the boy was carving a fishing hook big enough to catch a whale.

Tink saw her old friend, Peter Pan.

Taking a deep breath, Tink said, "Hello, Peter."

But Peter didn't seem to hear her. He continued to whistle and chip at the wood.

Tink flew a little bit closer. "Peter!" she exclaimed.

Peter kept on whistling and whittling.

Was he deaf? Or could he be angry with her? Tink wondered with a sudden shock. The thought had never occurred to her. She hovered, unsure what to do.

Then Terence took her hand. They flew up to Peter until they were just a few inches from his face. "Peter!" they both cried.

Peter lifted his head. When he saw them, a bright smile lit his face.

Tink smiled, too.

"Hello! What's this?" Peter said. He looked back and forth between the fairies.

"Two butterflies have come to visit me! Are you lost, butterflies?"

Tink's smile faded. She and Terence stared at Peter. *Butterflies?*

Tink thought, *Has he forgotten me already?*

Peter squinted at them and whistled low. "You're awful pretty. I just love butterflies," he said. "You'd make a fine addition to my collection. Let's see now, where are my pins?"

He began to search his pockets. As he did, small items fell onto the ground beneath his seat: a parrot's feather, a snail shell, a bit of string.

"Here it is!" he cried. He held up a straight pin with a colored bulb on the end. It was big enough to skewer a butterfly—

or a fairy—right through the middle.

"Now hold still," Peter said. Gripping the pin in one hand, he reached up to grab Tink and Terence with the other.

"Fly!" Terence screamed to Tink.

Just before Peter's stubby fingers closed around them, the fairies turned and fled toward the exit.

9

BUT AS THEY reached the roots of the jackfruit tree, they heard a whoop of laughter
behind them.

Tink stopped and glanced back over
her shoulder. Peter was clutching his stomach and shaking with laughter.

"Oh, Tink!" he gasped. "You should
have seen the looks on your faces.
Butterflies! Oh, I am funny. Oh, oh." He

bent over as another round of laughter seized him.

Terence, who had been just ahead of Tink, also stopped and turned. Frowning, he came to hover next to her. He had never met Peter Pan face to face before, and he was starting to think that he wasn't going to like him very much.

But Tink was smiling. It had only been a joke! Peter *did* remember her!

At last Peter stopped laughing. He bounded up to Tink and Terence, his eyes shining.

"Tink!" he cried. "It's awful great to see you. Where've you been hiding?"

"Hello, Peter," Tink replied. "Meet my friend Terence."

"A boy pixie! Fantastic!" Peter cried, turning to stare at Terence.

The grin on his face was so wide and enthusiastic that Terence's heart softened. The thing was, it was impossible not to like Peter Pan. He had the eagerness of a puppy, the cleverness of a fox, and the freedom of a lark—all rolled into one spry, redheaded boy.

"You'll never guess what I've got, Tink. Come see!" He said it as if Tink had been away for a mere few hours and had now come back to play.

Peter led Tink and Terence over to a corner of the hideout and pulled a wooden cigar box out of a hole in the wall. The word "Tarantula" was burned onto the lid. It was the name of the cigars Captain Hook liked to smoke. Peter had found the empty box on the beach, where Hook had thrown it away.

"I keep my most important things in my treasure chest," Peter explained to Terence, gesturing to the box. "The Lost Boys know better than to go poking around in here."

"Where are the Lost Boys?" Tink asked.

Peter thought for a moment. "They must still be hiding," he replied finally. "We were playing hide-and-seek in the forest yesterday. But when it was my turn to look, I spotted a bobcat stalking a rabbit. Course, I wanted to see if he caught him, so I followed them. I guess I forgot to go back and look for the boys."

"Do you think they're lost?" Terence asked.

Peter grinned. "Course they're lost!

They're the Lost Boys! I'll go find them later." He shrugged, then added, "Anyway, that bobcat never did catch the rabbit."

Peter lifted the lid of the cigar box. "Now . . ." Reaching inside, he took out a small object. He held it out toward Tink and Terence in the palm of his hand. It was yellowish white and shaped like a triangle, with razor-sharp edges that narrowed to a point.

Tink clasped her hands together. "Oh!" she gasped. "You got it!"

"What is it?" Terence asked.

"A shark's tooth," Peter replied, just a bit smugly. "Isn't it swell? I'm going to put it on a string and make a necklace."

"The first time I met Peter, he was trying to steal a shark's tooth," Tink explained to Terence.

"That's right!" exclaimed Peter. "I'd made a bet with the boys that I could steal a tooth from a live shark. I built a small raft out of birchwood and was paddling out to sea . . ."

From the way he began, Terence could tell that Peter had told this story many times before, and that he loved telling it.

"I had just paddled beyond the reef," Peter continued, "when I felt something bump the underside of my raft."

"The shark?" asked Terence.

Peter nodded. "He was looking for his lunch. But he didn't know that I was looking for him, too!"

"How did you plan to get his tooth?" Terence asked.

"I meant to stun him with my oar, then steal the tooth while he was out cold," said Peter. "But he was bigger than I'd thought, and before I knew it, he'd bitten my little raft right in half! I was sinking fast, and it looked like the end for me, when suddenly I heard a jingling sound over my head. I looked up and there was Tinker Bell. She yelled down at me . . ."

"'Fly, silly boy!'" Tink and Peter cried together. They laughed, remembering.

"But I didn't know how to fly," Peter told Terence. "So Tink taught me how, right then and there. She sprinkled some fairy dust on me, and before I knew it, I'd zipped up into the air, out of the shark's reach. Boy, was he mad!"

"So, you went back and got the shark tooth this time?" Tink asked Peter, pointing to the tooth in his hand.

Peter shrugged. "Naw. A mermaid gave

this to me. But now I'm going to go out and get the whole shark!" He pointed to the fishing pole and the wooden hook he'd been carving.

Tink and Peter both burst out laughing.

Terence smiled, watching them. He felt glad that Tink looked so happy. But it also made him sad. What if she decided to stay here in the forest with Peter?

Tink *was* happy. She had discovered that it wasn't so hard to see Peter, after all! She'd only needed a friend to help her find that out. She saw Terence's smile, and she smiled back at him.

Just then, Tink caught sight of something in the cigar box. Her eyes widened. "My hammer!" she exclaimed.

"I saved it for you, Tink," Peter said proudly. "I knew you'd be back for it."

Tink reached into the box and picked up the hammer. It fit perfectly in her hand. She tapped it lightly into the palm of her other hand, then closed her eyes and sighed. She felt as if she'd come home after a long, long trip.

Then, to Terence's joy and relief, Tink

turned to Peter and said, "It's been so good to see you, Peter. But we have to go back to the fairy kingdom now."

Peter looked at her in surprise. "What? Now? But what about hide-and-seek?"

Tink shook her head. She was glad to realize that she didn't want to stay, not for hide-and-seek or anything else. She wanted to get back to Pixie Hollow, back to her pots and pans. That was where she belonged.

Tink flew so close to Peter's face that he had to cross his eyes to see her. She kissed the bridge of his freckled nose. "I'll come back soon to visit," she promised. And she meant it.

Then, taking Terence's hand, she flew back out of the jackfruit tree and into the forest.

10

As Tink headed back to the fairy kingdom with Terence, one last thing was both-
ering her.

She didn't want all of Pixie Hollow to
know about the hammer and her trip to see
Peter. Enough hurtful gossip had already
spread through the kingdom. Tink didn't
want any more.

She wanted to ask Terence if he would

keep their trip to Peter's a secret between them. But before she could, he turned to her. "I don't think anyone else needs to know about this trip, do you?" he asked. "You've got your hammer back, and that's what matters."

Tink grinned and nodded. What a good friend Terence was.

"The only thing is," Terence said, "how will we convince everyone that you have your talent back?"

Tink thought for a moment. "I have an idea," she said.

Putting on a burst of speed, Tink raced Terence all the way back to Pixie Hollow.

When they got to the Home Tree, Tink went straight to Queen Ree's quarters.

One of the queen's attendants opened

the door. "Tink, welcome," the attendant said when she saw her.

"I've come to fix the queen's bathtub," Tink told her.

Terence, who was standing behind Tink, grinned. Tink was clever. This was the perfect way to prove that her talent was back. Terence didn't doubt that Tink could

fix the tub. She was the best pots-and-pans fairy in the kingdom.

But the attendant hesitated. Everyone had heard about Tink and her talent. She wanted to refuse to let Tink fix it.

Just then, Ree stepped forward. She had heard Tink's request. "Come in, Tink," she said.

"I've come to fix your bathtub," Tink repeated to the queen.

Ree looked at Tink. In Tink's blue eyes, she saw a fierce certainty that hadn't been there the day before, when they'd talked in the gazebo.

Ree nodded. "Take Tink to the bath-tub," she told her attendant.

The attendant looked startled, but she turned and began to lead Tink away.

Just before Tink left, Terence grabbed her hand. "Good luck," he said.

Tink held up her hammer and gave his hand a squeeze. "I don't need it!" she said.

This is the end of
THE TROUBLE WITH TINK.
Turn the page to read
TINK, NORTH OF NEVER LAND.

Tink,
North
of
Never Land

Tink, North of Never Land

WRITTEN BY
KIKI THORPE

ILLUSTRATED BY
JUDITH HOLMES CLARKE,
ADRIENNE BROWN & CHARLES PICKENS

A STEPPING STONE BOOK™
RANDOM HOUSE 🏠 NEW YORK

1

"Last one to the meadow is a gooseberry!" Tinker Bell cried. "Terence, you don't stand a chance."

With a flap of her wings, Tink took off flying. It was early morning in Pixie Hollow. The air was cool and fresh. Below her, dew on the grass sparkled in the sunlight.

As she passed a patch of larkspur, the meadow came into view. She could see harvest fairies carrying armfuls of buttercups. A herd of dairy mice nosed through the grass, looking for seeds.

Tink glanced back at her friend Terence, a fairy-dust-talent sparrow man. He was way behind her. She turned and began to fly backward.

"A one-winged moth could fly faster than you!" she teased.

Terence grinned. But as he opened his mouth to reply, he saw something hurtling through the air. It was headed right for Tink!

"Tink!" he yelled. "Look out!"

Tink looked up. She dodged out of the way just in time.

As the thing zoomed past, Tink realized it was Twire, a scrap-metal-recovery fairy. Twire's arms were wrapped around a big metal object. She was struggling to stay aloft.

A second later, her wings gave out. Twire plummeted toward the ground.

"Twire!" Tink cried. She and Terence dove after her. But Twire was falling too fast. They couldn't catch up.

At the last second, Twire let go of the metal object. It slammed to the ground. Twire crashed next to it, just missing a dairy mouse. The mouse took off running with a frightened squeak.

Twire flipped once, head over heels. She came to a stop flat on her back.

Tink and Terence rushed over. "Are you all right?" Terence asked.

The scrap-metal fairy rose shakily to

her feet. Her elbows and knees were scraped, and one of her wings was bent. But her glow was bright with excitement.

"Look what I found," she said breathlessly, and pointed at the object. It was round and made of brass, with a glass front like a clock's. But instead of two hands, it had a single thin needle as long as a fairy's arm.

"What is it?" asked Terence.

Twire shook her head. "I don't know. I found it on the beach. But just look at all that brass!"

Twire's talent was collecting bits of unwanted metal and melting them down so that they could be remade into useful things. On a normal day, she picked up a few scraps of tin or a bucket that was rusted beyond repair. She rarely found such a large solid piece of brass.

Terence nudged the object with his foot. "It's awfully heavy," he said. "Why didn't you use fairy dust to carry it?" A sprinkling of dust could make almost anything float. Fairies often used it to carry heavy things.

"I did. I guess I didn't use enough," Twire admitted. She looked sheepish. Twire always used as little fairy dust as possible. She couldn't help it, really. As a scrap-metal-recovery fairy, she was thrifty by nature.

Tink said, "I've seen one of these before. It's called a compass. Clumsies use them to keep from getting lost."

"Clumsies" was the fairies' name for

humans. Tink knew about Clumsies from her adventures with Peter Pan. For years she had lived in his hideout and run wild with the Lost Boys. Those were some of her favorite memories.

"Compasses are very useful," she added, remembering what Peter had told her.

Twire looked dismayed. If the compass was still useful, she couldn't melt it down. "But this one's no good," she blurted out. "See how tarnished the brass is?"

"The brass doesn't matter. It's the needle that's important," Tink told her. "Whichever way you turn the compass, the needle always points north."

To show them, she began to turn the

compass on the ground. Terence gave her a hand. They pushed the compass in a full circle. But instead of pointing north, the needle turned right along with the compass.

"It's broken!" Twire cried gleefully.

"I can fix it," Tink said.

Twire scowled at Tink. Tink met her gaze. Although the two were friends, they were often at odds. Tink always wanted to fix broken things. Twire, on the other hand, always wanted to melt them down.

For a moment, the two fairies glared at each other. Then, with a sigh, Twire said, "All right, Tink, it's yours." She took a last longing look at the brass and flew off to search for more metal.

When Twire was gone, Terence leaned in and pretended to examine the compass. He didn't really care about it, though. He just wanted to be close to Tink.

Terence liked Tink. He admired her dimples and her springy blond ponytail. He marveled at her talent for fixing pots and pans. In fact, he thought it was the best talent next to fairy dust. He loved Tink's smile, but he didn't mind when she frowned. Frowns were part of Tink, too. Above all, Terence liked that Tink was always herself. There was no other fairy like her.

Now Tink placed her hands on the compass. Her wings quivered with excitement. She had never fixed any-thing like it before. But she knew she could. She was the best pots-and-pans fairy in Pixie Hollow.

"Want me to help you take the compass to your workshop?" Terence asked. Tink nodded.

Terence sprinkled the compass with fairy dust. Then he remembered Twire's crash landing and added an extra pinch for safety. Together, Tink and Terence lifted it into the air.

They reached Tink's workshop, carrying the compass between them. But the fairy-sized door was a problem. When they tried to push the compass through, it got stuck. They shoved with all their strength. But it was wedged in tight.

"Now what?" asked Terence. He

slumped against the brass side of the compass.

Tink thought for a moment. "I'll make it shrink," she said at last. The magic would be tricky. It wasn't usual pots-and-pans magic. But Tink was sure she could do it.

She threw more fairy dust on the compass. Then she closed her eyes. Terence stood by, ready to lend a hand.

Terence is sweet, Tink thought. *He would do anything to help a friend.* She recalled the time he had gone with her to Peter Pan's hideout to get a hammer she'd left there. He had known, without being told, that Tink needed his help. And he'd offered it without being asked.

He's also very talented, thought Tink.

He can measure out cupfuls of fairy dust without losing a speck. And he has a nice smile. His smile sparkles.

With a start, Tink realized that she wasn't thinking about the compass. She was thinking about Terence.

Tink opened her eyes. She was looking right at him. Terence smiled.

Tink frowned and looked away. She turned so that her back was to him.

"Can I help, Tink?" Terence asked.

"I don't need help." Tink wished he weren't hovering so close. In fact, she suddenly wished he weren't there at all.

She closed her eyes again. This time, she thought only about the compass. She imagined it getting smaller, the metal contracting, compressing. . . .

The compass began to shrink. It was only a smidgen, but Terence was ready. As soon as he saw it change, he gave a hard shove. With a screech of metal against metal, the compass rolled free and into the room.

At once, Terence knew he'd made a mistake. The compass was rolling straight toward Tink's worktable, with its teetering pile of pots and pans. He darted forward to stop it.

As he did, his wings swept a small silver bowl off Tink's shelf.

The bowl spun across the floor, right into the path of—

"No!" Tink cried.

Crunch! The compass rolled over the bowl, which crumpled like paper.

Tink pushed past Terence. She picked up the crushed bowl and cradled it in her hands.

Terence began to apologize. "I'd fly backward—"

"Look what you've done, Terence!" Tink exploded. She was shaking with anger. "Wherever I turn, you're under-wing. If you really wanted to help me, you'd leave me alone!"

Terence drew back as if he'd been slapped. Without a word, he turned and flew away.

2

TINK WATCHED TERENCE leave. She half hoped he would turn around and come back. But he didn't. Soon he was out of sight.

She frowned and tugged her bangs. Perhaps she'd spoken a little harshly, and a little quickly.

"But Terence *is* always in my way," she complained, trying to convince herself. "I can't even turn around without tripping over him. And now look what a mess he's made."

She examined the crumpled silver bowl. Flattened as it was, it looked more like a plate.

"There, there," Tink murmured. "I'll have you put right in no time."

She ran her fingers lovingly over the silver. Tink adored anything made of metal. But this bowl was particularly special. It was the first thing she'd ever fixed as a pots-and-pans fairy, just after she'd arrived in Never Land. She hadn't been sure she *could* fix it. And she was so pleased at the way it had finally turned out.

As soon as her tinker's hammer was in her hands, she relaxed. Before long,

she was lost in her work. She almost
managed to forget all about Terence.

⟳⟲⟳

As Terence flew through Pixie Hollow,
he hardly saw where he was going. Tink's
words kept running through his mind.
He'd never known she felt that way. He'd

been hanging around her for years. Had he been a bother the whole time?

"I'll leave Tink alone from now on," Terence vowed. The idea made him sad. But what else could he do? She didn't want him around.

These heavy thoughts weighed Terence down, until he was flying just inches above the ground. His feet brushed the tips of grass blades as he flew over them.

Without noticing how he'd gotten there, Terence came to Minnow Lake. The lake was really no more than a puddle. But to the tiny folk of Pixie Hollow, it seemed vast. Although they couldn't swim, many fairies and sparrow men went there to enjoy the sunshine or just to dip their feet in the cool water.

Terence flew straight over the lake. His toes kicked up a spray. His boots got soaked and he didn't even feel it.

Suddenly, something whipped by him in a blur. Terence looked up and saw the water fairy Silvermist. She was gliding across the top of the lake on one foot, as graceful as an ice-skater. Her long blue-black hair waved behind her like a banner.

Silvermist skated up to Terence, smiling. Right away, she noticed his gloomy expression.

"Why, Terence, what's wrong? You look as if you lost your best friend."

Terence looked at her in surprise. How did she know?

Silvermist didn't know. But like all

water fairies, she was very sensitive. She could tell Terence was hurting.

"I know what would cheer you up. Water-skating!" she said. "Want to join me?"

Terence watched as she twirled. "Sure, but I don't see how," he replied. "Only water talents can walk on water."

"Wrong!" said Silvermist. She spun on her toes and sped away.

Moments later, she returned. In her hands was a pair of green sandals with wide flat soles. She handed them to Terence.

"Put these skimmers on," Silvermist instructed. "They're made from lily pads. They'll keep you afloat."

Terence eyed the lily pad skimmers

doubtfully. But he strapped them on over his boots. Gingerly, he set one foot, then the other, down on the surface of the lake.

He was standing on water!

"Whoops!"

Terence's feet slipped out from under him. He caught himself with his wings before he fell into the lake.

"They take some getting used to," said Silvermist. "Try walking. It's easier than standing still. You can use your wings for balance."

Terence took a careful step. He was surprised to find that the water was springy. It felt like walking on deep moss.

He took another step. Then he took

three giant steps, flapping his wings in between. Each time he set his foot down, it bounced off the water. Soon he was bounding around the lake.

For the first time since that morning, Terence smiled.

Tink stretched out the crick in her back and sighed happily. She had worked hard all afternoon. After she'd fixed the bowl, she had started on the compass.

"At this rate, I'll have it working again by tomorrow," she said.

She stood and flew out of her workshop. Outside, she headed toward the orchard. "I'll go pick a cherry," Tink said. "I'm feeling kind of hungry."

She followed the bank of Havendish Stream. As she passed Minnow Lake, Tink heard laughter.

That's Terence's laugh, she thought.

Suddenly, she remembered what had happened that morning. *Maybe I was a little mean,* thought Tink. After all, the bowl had been easy to fix. Tink shrugged. *Oh, well.* She'd give him a friendly smile and show him that all was forgiven.

She flew to the lake and landed at the edge. There was Terence, skipping across the surface of the lake like a water strider. Silvermist skated along behind him.

Tink waved at them from the shore. Silvermist didn't see her, but Terence

did. He was about to wave back. Then he remembered his vow. He kept his arms at his sides.

Tink frowned. Hadn't they seen her? She waved again. This time she was sure Terence glanced in her direction. But he turned and skipped away.

Tink lowered her arm. "Well," she said at last. "I'm glad Terence found someone to play with, at least."

And with a toss of her ponytail, she went on her way.

3

THE NEXT MORNING, Terence was up
early. As the first rays of sunlight
warmed Pixie Hollow, he filled a gunny-
sack with fairy dust. Then he set off to
make his rounds. His job as a dust talent
was to make sure all the fairies and sparrow men of Pixie Hollow had enough
dust to do magic.

As he flew, Terence tried not to
think about Tinker Bell. But it wasn't

easy. He passed cornflowers the color of her eyes and buttercups as golden as her hair. By the time he came upon the light-talent fairy Iridessa, Terence had been unsuccessfully not-thinking about Tink for more than an hour.

At that moment, Iridessa was head-first in a large day lily. The lily glowed from within like a giant orange lantern. Terence gently tapped Iridessa's foot to let her know he was there.

Iridessa shrieked and popped her head up. She had yellow pollen in her hair. More pollen was streaked across one cheek.

"Terence! You could scare the fairy dust off someone, sneaking up like that!"

"Wouldn't you know it?" Terence

said with a sigh. "And it's my job to put the fairy dust *on* fairies." He scooped a cupful of dust from the sack and poured it over Iridessa. She shivered lightly as the dust settled on her.

"So, why are you collecting pollen?" Terence asked. "Have you turned into a garden fairy?"

"Come on," she said to Terence. "I'll show you."

Iridessa grabbed the basket of pollen. She led Terence to a nearby clearing and told him, "Take a seat."

For a moment, Iridessa hovered, focusing. Then she held up her hands. She began to pull sunlight out of the air.

Terence looked on in wonder. Every fairy and sparrow man had a magical talent, and Terence loved his best of all. But he was always amazed by the magic other fairies could do.

When Iridessa was done, she and Terence were sitting in a halo of darkness. It was like the circle of light a campfire casts on a moonless night. Only instead of a bright spot in the darkness, it was a dark spot in the daylight.

"Amazing!" Terence said.

Iridessa glanced at him. The sunlight she had gathered sat in balls at her feet. "That's not even the good part. But I need darkness, or you won't be able to see what I'm about to do."

She took some of the sunlight and formed it into a bubble. Then she filled the bubble with pollen from her basket. She drew her arm back and threw it into the air as hard as she could.

Terence watched the bubble of light travel up, up, up. It burst with a pop. Golden pollen rained down. It looked like fireworks. But there was no fire—only pollen, light, and magic.

Terence thought, *I wish Tink could*

see this. "It's brilliant!" he told Iridessa.

She beamed at the compliment and threw two more pollen-filled bubbles into the air. They burst in golden sprays of light.

"Wait!" Terence sprang to his feet. "I have an idea. Try using fairy dust."

Iridessa formed another ball of light. This time, Terence filled it with dust from his sack.

The fairy-dust-filled bubble floated out of Iridessa's hands even before she could throw it. It rose all the way up to the edge of the darkness.

Just when Terence thought the bubble would drift into daylight and disappear, it exploded. Blue, violet, green, yellow, orange, red—the light shimmered

with the bright colors of the rainbow.

Terence and Iridessa watched in awe, the sparkles reflected in their eyes.

"Got it!" Tink cried.

She stepped back and watched the compass needle swing around. She was sure she'd finally fixed it. As Tink turned the compass, the needle pointed north. She'd fixed it, all right.

She stretched her arms and sighed with pleasure. How she enjoyed seeing a job done right! She turned the compass a few more times, just to admire her work.

Gradually, though, Tink became aware that something was missing. She checked to make sure she had her tinker's hammer. Then she checked her other tools. They were all there.

She looked around her workshop. Everything seemed to be in its place. The extra rivets were in their hanging basket. The little jars of glue lined the windowsill in a neat row. The silver bowl was back on its shelf, right where it had been before Terence knocked it off.

Terence! Suddenly, Tink realized that *he* was what was missing. Usually he stopped by to visit. But she hadn't seen him all day.

He must be busy. After all, he has work to do, too, Tink thought.

"I'll drop by the fairy dust mill and see how he is," she said. The mill was where Terence spent most of his time.

Tink flew out the door. She followed the hill that sloped down toward the mill, which sat on the bank of Havendish Stream.

She flew through the mill's double doors. Inside, it was cool and dim. Tink saw several fairies and sparrow men at work. But Terence wasn't among them.

Tink flew back outside. She was surprised at how disappointed she felt.

As she made her way back to the Home Tree, Tink saw a spark of light float up from a nearby field. Another spark followed.

Fireflies? she wondered. No, that couldn't be right. Fireflies only came out at night. Tink flew over to take a look.

When she reached the field, she stopped and stared. In the center was a small clearing. Though the sun shone brightly overhead, the clearing was as dark as night. Within the darkness, bursts of light bloomed like flowers.

Looking more closely, she made out two tiny figures on the ground. One was her friend Iridessa. Tink strained her eyes, then blinked in surprise. The other one was Terence! With each new explosion, he and Iridessa clapped and cheered.

Tink hovered at the edge of the darkness, feeling strangely left out.

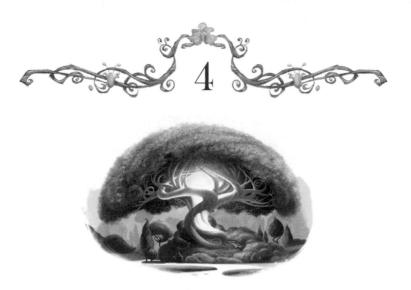

4

THAT EVENING, TINK hurried to the courtyard of the Home Tree. The sun was
already setting. Any minute, the story
would begin. She didn't want to be late.

Dinner had just ended. It was time
for the story-talent fairies to spin their
tales. That night, it was Tor's turn, and
Tor was one of Tink's favorite story-
tellers. He knew more about pixie lore
than most fairies put together.

The courtyard was filling with fairies and sparrow men. Tink looked around for Terence. They usually sat together during stories.

More and more fairies arrived. They settled onto toadstools around the courtyard.

Tink tugged her bangs. Where was Terence? If he didn't get there soon, all the good seats would be taken!

On the other side of the courtyard, Terence caught sight of Tink. The seat next to him was empty, and he wanted to call her over.

But we aren't friends anymore, he reminded himself.

As Terence hesitated, he heard someone call his name. He looked around.

Rosetta, a garden fairy, was hovering behind him.

She pointed to the seat next to Terence. "Is someone sitting here?"

Terence shook his head.

Rosetta sat down. She carefully smoothed her rose-petal skirt. She fluffed her hair. Then she crossed her dainty ankles and folded her hands in her lap. With her long auburn curls, rosy cheeks, and elegant wings, Rosetta was one of the prettiest fairies in all of Pixie Hollow. She knew it, too.

When she was finally settled, she turned to Terence. It was then that she noticed his sad expression.

"Ah!" Rosetta gasped in horror.

Terence leaped into the air. "What?

What is it?" He thought maybe a fire ant had crawled onto his toadstool.

"You shouldn't frown like that. Your face could get stuck," Rosetta told him gravely. "It happened to a fairy I know. Her face got stuck in a frown, and after that she always looked as sour as a stinkbug. That's why I always smile. If my face ever gets stuck, at least I'll know I'll always look good." To prove her point, she flashed a brilliant grin.

Rosetta's advice was lost on Terence. He never thought much about how he looked. He did notice Rosetta's smile, though. It was so charming, he couldn't help smiling back.

At that very moment, Tink finally spotted Terence. Her mouth fell open in surprise. Terence hadn't saved her a seat after all. He was sitting with Rosetta. And they looked very happy to be together!

Tink felt a lump in the pit of her stomach. But before she could do anything, a hush settled over the crowd. The story was about to begin. Quickly, Tink looked around. All the seats were taken.

"*Pssst.* Tink!"

Fawn, an animal-talent fairy, waved at her. "You can share with me," Fawn whispered.

Tink flew down and squeezed herself in next to Fawn. As she did, she noticed a stinky smell.

"What's that smell?" she whispered to Fawn.

"Oh, it's probably me! I was playing

tag with some skunks," Fawn told her. "Didn't get a chance to take a bath."

Tink nodded and held her breath. At least she had a seat.

The storyteller Tor alighted in the center of the courtyard. He looked around with twinkling eyes. Then he began, "Long, long ago, before the Home Tree, even before Mother Dove, there was the Pixie Dust Tree."

Tink let out a small sigh. She knew the story of the Pixie Dust Tree well. It was one of her favorites.

"In those days, Pixie Hollow was a great land," Tor went on. "It stretched for miles. It covered mountains, forests, and rivers."

Tink mouthed the next words along

with the storyteller: *Too many years ago to count.*

"The Pixie Dust Tree stood at the center of it all," said Tor. "The dust flowed endlessly from deep within its trunk. And because the dust was plentiful, so was the fairies' magic. . . ."

As Tor spoke, the Pixie Dust Tree seemed to take shape before the fairies' eyes. Tink saw every detail, from its spiraling branches to its sturdy roots. She could hear its leaves rustle. She could feel the breeze from the gusts of pixie dust that rose from its center. That was the magic of story-talent fairies. Whatever they described became, in that moment, real.

Tor's story wove a spell around his

audience. The fairies saw Pixie Hollow as it once had been: purple mountains, crystal-clear streams, fields of sunflowers stretching as far as the eye could see. And everywhere, fairies flying, playing, and living happily.

Then, suddenly, the scene darkened. An evil force threatened the fairies' world. No storyteller would say its name out loud. They were afraid of calling it back again. So in Tor's story, it appeared as a black cloud casting its shadow over Pixie Hollow.

The fairies in the story knew their world was in danger. They used every bit of magic they had to protect it. But in the end, they couldn't save everything.

They watched helplessly as the dark

cloud swallowed the Pixie Dust Tree.

As brave as Tink was, she always found that part of the story hard to bear. Without thinking, she closed her eyes and reached out her hand to Terence.

Her hand closed on nothing. Tink's eyes opened. She'd forgotten. Terence wasn't sitting next to her.

Tink looked around. Fawn's eyes were wet. So were the eyes of other fairies.

"But in its place, the Home Tree grew," Tor told them. "Fairies came from all over Pixie Hollow to live in the tree and make it their home. It brought the Never fairies together. And we found Mother Dove, who gave us fairy dust again."

The fairies saw the image of Mother

Dove. Her feathers shimmered. After the Pixie Dust Tree had been destroyed, fairies had learned to make dust from the magical feathers Mother Dove shed.

"The Pixie Dust Tree is long gone," Tor told them. "But a bit of its dust still remains. It hangs in a cloud just over the cliffs on the Northern Shore of Never Land. You can see it on certain nights."

A sparkling cloud seemed to hang in the air around the listening fairies. As they watched, it began to fade. Finally, it disappeared.

For a moment, the crowd was silent. Then one fairy sighed. Another stretched her wings. The spell was broken. The story was over.

The crowd began to rise from their

seats. A few of the music talents struck up a melody. Some of the fairies stayed to dance. Others headed back to the tearoom, hoping to find dessert.

Tink heard Fawn's stomach growl. "Sad stories always make me hungry," Fawn explained. "Come with me to the tearoom?"

"Sure," said Tink. She glanced at Terence and added, "Maybe we should invite Terence and Rosetta, too."

"Good idea," said Fawn. "Rosetta hates to miss dessert."

Together they flew toward Terence and Rosetta. But just as they reached them, the music fairies began to play a lively tune.

Rosetta sprang up from her seat.

"This is my favorite song. Let's dance, Terence!"

She grabbed his hands and pulled him into the air. In the wink of an eye, the two had danced away.

5

Tink was so surprised, her glow sputtered. She watched Terence and Rosetta twirl through the air. They didn't so much as glance in her direction.

I didn't want their company anyway! she thought. *I have better things to do than watch two silly fairies dance.*

Ignoring Fawn's surprised look, she whirled around and stormed off to her workshop.

Inside, she slammed the door behind her. When that didn't make her feel better, she kicked over the basket of rivets. They rolled to every corner of her tidy workshop, which only made Tink's temper worse.

"Every time I see Terence, he ignores me!" she fumed. She paced in the air.

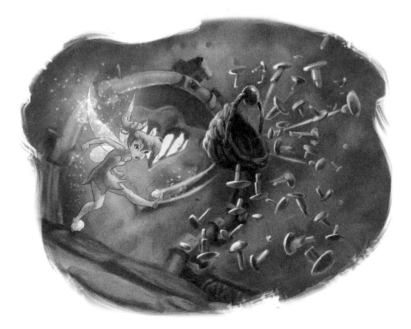

"Why, he practically goes out of his way to avoid me. And he hasn't been by to visit since . . . since . . ."

Oh.

Tink sat down with a thump. Finally, it dawned on her: she'd told Terence to leave her alone, and that was exactly what he was doing.

All the anger went out of her like air from a bellows. Within seconds, it was replaced by regret.

I haven't been very nice to Terence, she thought with a sigh. Her shoulders slumped. Losing a friend felt terrible.

But she wasn't one to mope for long. In Tink's opinion, problems were like broken pots. There wasn't one that couldn't be fixed. She was, after all, the best pots-and-pans fairy in Pixie Hollow. Surely she could come up with a solution.

A moment later, she'd thought of one.

"I'll win back his friendship!" she exclaimed. "I'll show everyone what a good friend I am." The idea made her spring into the air with excitement.

"But how will I do it?" She began to pace again.

It never occurred to Tink to say "I'm sorry." Only Clumsies said that. She might have said, "I'd fly backward if I could." But that didn't occur to Tink, either. She was too busy thinking of bigger, flashier ways to show that she cared.

"I'll give him a present," she said.

"Something rare and wonderful." Her mind swirled with possibilities. A pirates' gold doubloon? Or a bunch of Never blooms with blossoms that never wilted?

Tink shook her head. Those things were marvelous, of course. But what would Terence care for a flower or a gold coin? No, she wanted to give him something that was right only for him.

Terence is a dust talent, she mused. *He loves fairy dust as much as I love pots and pans.* But she couldn't give him fairy dust. He already had all the dust he could ever want.

Or did he? Tink remembered the end of Tor's story: "The Pixie Dust Tree is long gone. But a bit of its dust still remains. It hangs in a cloud just over the cliffs on the Northern Shore of Never Land."

That was it! Pixie dust was just like fairy dust, only it came from a tree instead of Mother Dove. She could bring Terence dust from the Pixie Dust Tree!

Tink imagined how Terence's face would look when she gave him the last pixie dust in the world. How impressed he would be!

The Northern Shore was far from Pixie Hollow. It might take her days to get there, and the journey was sure to be rough. But the challenge only made Tink more excited.

"I'll leave tonight," she said. "I'll

need to bring food. And extra fairy dust to fly—"

Tink's eyes fell on the compass. Of course. She could take it with her. It would point her right to the Northern Shore. How wise she'd been to save the compass from Twire's scrap pile!

She began to pack, piling things on top of the compass—a sweater, a canteen, a sack of dried blueberries, a wool blanket, her spare dagger, a waterproof pouch to store her fairy dust in, some biscuits, a tin cup, a bag of tea . . .

Tink stepped back. The heap of things towered nearly to her chest. How in Never Land was she going to carry it all?

She snapped her fingers. "A balloon carrier!"

Balloon carriers were large fairy-dust-filled balloons with hanging baskets. Fairies used them to carry heavy loads. Some were big enough to carry fifty fairies. Others were quite small, just the right size for a fairy, a compass, and a few other odds and ends.

She knew she shouldn't take a balloon carrier without telling anyone. But she was afraid that if Queen Clarion heard of her plan, she would forbid Tink to go. *Besides*, Tink reasoned, *if other fairies knew, it might ruin the surprise for Terence.* Fairies were terrible at keeping secrets.

"I'll be gone for just a few days," she said. "I'm sure the others won't even miss it."

Tink knew that the laundry fairies kept small balloon carriers anchored to roots inside the laundry room. The problem was getting one without anyone noticing.

"I'll have to borrow it after everyone goes to bed," she whispered to herself.

So, drawing her little stool up to the window, Tink settled down to wait.

6

THE MOON WAS high in the sky. The Home Tree was dark and silent. Even the fire-flies that lit Pixie Hollow at night had blinked out.

As quietly as possible, Tink loaded the balloon carrier. Then she picked up the carrier cord and rose into the air. She circled the Home Tree, careful not to snag the balloon on low branches.

She flew over the barn where the

dairy mice slept, and continued up, until she was above the tree line. She skimmed along the tops of the trees. Every few minutes, she darted back to look at the compass. She loved to see the needle pointing north, telling her exactly which way to go.

She'd been flying for a quarter of an hour when she looked down. Her heart sank. She was just crossing Havendish Stream.

At this rate, it will take me weeks to reach the Northern Shore! she thought.

But as luck would have it, the wind shifted in Tink's direction. She felt the carrier bumping against her heels.

Tink climbed into the basket. She let the wind speed her along. In no time, she had reached the edge of Pixie Hollow. Never Land's forest spread out below her like a great dark sea.

A moth flew up to the basket. It danced around Tink, drawn by her glow. She waved her arms, and the moth flew away.

Tink leaned back. High overhead, stars winked in the black sky. The basket gently rocked her. Her eyelids grew heavy.

Within moments, she fell fast asleep.

Tink awoke with a start. The balloon had stopped moving.

She peeked over the side. The ropes that held the balloon to the basket were tangled in the branches of a large oak. The balloon must have drifted too low while she had been sleeping.

Tink climbed out of the basket and landed on a branch. She began to tug at the ropes.

Something snuffled behind her. She

whirled around. A pair of red eyes stared at her from the darkness.

Tink gasped and sprang into the air. Through the leaves of the tree, she could see more creatures in the branches around her. Each way Tink turned, she saw another pair of glowing eyes. She was trapped!

One of the creatures began to move along a branch toward her. Taking a deep breath, Tink flared her glow like a flame, hoping to scare it away.

It worked. The creature hissed and retreated to the other end of the branch. By the light of her brightened glow, Tink saw the long, pointed nose of a possum.

Tink tried to remember everything she knew about possums. They didn't

eat fairies—did they? Fawn had once told her a story about a possum, though Tink couldn't recall the details. Oh, why hadn't she paid more attention!

One thing Tink did know was that she was still in trouble. The possums were bigger than she was, and she had dropped into their home. If they felt threatened, Tink was in danger.

Cautiously, Tink landed again on the branch. Keeping an eye on the largest possum, she began to pull at the tangled ropes. Every time a possum moved, she flared her glow.

Just as Tink grabbed the last rope, she heard a low growl. The largest possum had made up her mind. She didn't want Tink in her tree.

The possum bared her sharp teeth. Tink gave a desperate tug, and the rope came free. Quickly, she grabbed the carrier cord. She darted toward an opening in the branches, dragging the balloon.

The noise of the balloon crashing through the leaves startled the possums. They drew back just enough to make a path. Tink flew out of the tree and kept on going.

High above the forest, Tink came to a stop. She climbed into the basket and huddled there, shaking. Flaring her glow had used up all her energy.

Tink drifted in the balloon. She didn't care where the breeze took her, as long as it was away from the oak tree. But luck was once again on her side.

When she checked the compass, she saw she was still headed north.

For the rest of the night, Tink pinched herself to stay awake. She was afraid to doze off again. When the wind changed direction, she got out and flew. Always she followed the compass needle to stay on course.

At last she saw a thin red glow on the horizon. Tink guided the carrier down to the edge of a small clearing. She tied the cord to a tree root to anchor it.

Under the shelter of a wild rosebush, she unrolled her blanket. She plucked a blossom to use as a pillow and curled up on a leaf.

Finally, she slept.

7

THE SUN HAD been up for hours when Tink opened her eyes. She heard the sound of waves breaking on a beach.

I must be near the ocean, she thought sleepily.

In an instant, she was wide-awake. The sound could mean only one thing. She had reached the Nothern Shore!

But how was that possible? Tink wondered. Surely the Northern Shore was still at least a day's flight away. She darted up into the air, until she could see over the tops of the trees. Blue-green water shimmered in the distance.

"The ocean!" cried Tink.

She raced back to her camp and checked the compass needle. It pointed toward the water. She did a joyful little dance. She *had* made it to the Northern Shore!

Quickly, she ate a dried blueberry and washed it down with water from the canteen. Then she packed everything into the basket and took off through the forest.

The sound of the surf grew louder. Up ahead, she caught glimpses of blue sky between the trees.

"Almost there!"

She emerged into sunlight. For a moment, she hovered, blinking. After the shady forest, the brightness was blinding. Over the splash of the waves, she could hear a different noise, like a melody.

It sounds as if someone is singing, thought Tink.

As her eyes got used to the light, Tink looked around. Soft white sand stretched a mile in each direction. Blue water gently lapped the shore. Coconut palms rustled in the breeze.

Tink thought, *This beach seems familiar. . . .*

Then she saw it. Straight out at sea, a large seaweed-covered rock rose from the water. A lovely woman sat on top. Her long tail with glistening scales curled down one side of the rock.

Tink's heart sank. The creature on the rock was a mermaid. And the song she heard was a mermaid's song. She hadn't reached the Northern Shore at all. This was Mermaid Lagoon, less than an hour's flight from Pixie Hollow.

Tink flew circles of fury. "But how?" she wailed. She had checked the compass over and over again. Always she'd gone north, in the direction the needle pointed. So how had she come to Mermaid Lagoon? Everyone in Never Land knew that it was on the opposite side of the island—

Tink dropped to the ground. How

could she have been so stupid? Of course, a compass would be worthless on Never Land. For although a compass always pointed north, the island turned in whatever direction it wanted. Unlike most islands, Never Land floated freely in the ocean.

The night before, as Tink had flown doggedly north, Never Land had turned itself around. So she had ended up back where she'd started.

"Northern Shore. What a stupid name!" Tink growled. "Whoever thought it up should be pinched black and blue. And as for this piece of junk—"

In a fit of rage, Tink hauled the compass out to sea and threw it in. With a splash, it vanished beneath the waves.

Tink flew back to shore and flung herself down on the sand. She shook off the urge to cry.

"I won't give up," she told herself. "I'll get to the Northern Shore if I have to fly for a week."

Tink's will was like the pots she fixed—it was made of iron. She had never failed before. And she wouldn't this time, either.

Her mind made up, Tink stood and reached for the carrier cord. But it wasn't there. She spun around. The carrier was nowhere in sight.

Looking up, she spotted it high in the sky. In her rage over the compass, she had forgotten to tie it down. As Tink watched, the carrier drifted over the top of a towering palm tree and was gone.

Tink clutched her head in horror. She'd lost an entire balloon carrier! What would the queen say if she knew? What would Terence think?

But the carrier wasn't all she'd lost. Her food was gone, and so was her water. She'd have to find her own from here on. Luckily, she had kept her fairy dust with her. Tink checked her supply. She figured she had four days' worth, at least.

Now she was more determined than ever to find the dust from the Pixie Dust Tree. She had to prove that her journey had been worth it.

She set off flying through the woods. It was easier traveling by day.

She knew that as long as she kept Torth Mountain on her right, she was headed the right way.

Tink flew all morning. When her shoulders ached too much to go on, she stopped beside a small spring. She took a long drink of cool water. Then she sat back to rest.

She thought about the journey ahead. She would have to pass through miles of forest. *Dark, shadowy forest,* Tink thought with a shiver, *where I could run into a tree snake or an owl or some other scary creature. A monster that could snap a fairy up in a single bite . . .*

Tink shook her head. What was wrong with her? She had never been afraid of the forest before. Back in the days of Peter Pan, she had lived for adventures like this.

But so many things had gone wrong this time—the possums, the compass, the balloon carrier. She had made many mistakes. Maybe she had been wrong to come on this journey by herself.

Tink stood and brushed away the thought. "I just need something to eat," she told herself. "After a snack, I'll feel fit as a fiddlehead fern again."

Downstream, she spotted a gooseberry bush heavy with plump glossy berries. She flew over to it.

Tink was wrestling with a gooseberry, trying to tug it from its stem, when she suddenly had the feeling she was being watched.

She dropped the berry and ducked into the bush. Her encounter with the possums was fresh in her mind. She scanned the forest. Not a single leaf moved. Even the air was still. There was nothing—

No, wait! There! A pair of fox ears poked up from behind a hollow log.

Tink gasped. A fox *would* eat a fairy if it was hungry enough. Her muscles tensed. She prepared to dart away.

The ears lifted. But they weren't attached to a fox. Beneath them was the face of a boy.

"Slightly!" Tink cried.

Slightly held his finger to his lips. But it was too late. There was a flash of green as something swooped down from above.

And before them stood Peter Pan.

8

TINK GRINNED. EVEN though they'd had
their ups and downs, she was always glad
to see Peter. She came out from the bush
and flew to meet him.

"Tink!" Peter exclaimed. "You're
just in time." It had been weeks since
they'd last seen each other, but Peter
acted as if Tink had been away for minutes. "I was about to find Slightly," he
told her.

"Were not!" came the voice from behind the log. "At least, not until Tink gave me away." Slightly poked his head up to scowl at Tink.

Peter reached over and tapped Slightly on the head. "And now you're *it*."

At the word "it," there was a rustle in the bushes. Cubby, Nibs, and the Twins came out from their hiding places.

Tink looked over the boys in their ragged animal-fur suits. Someone was missing.

"Where's Tootles?" she asked Peter.

Peter shrugged. "Sometimes he falls asleep." He jumped onto a tree branch and leaned out past the leaves. "Tootles! Tootles, come out!" he called.

There was no reply.

"Tootles! Tootles!" the Lost Boys called. But still they heard nothing.

Suddenly, one of the Twins cried out. "Peter, look! Tootles's footprints go to here. Then they disappear!"

Peter leaped down to study the tracks. He whistled low. "Disappeared right into thin air. There's only one thing that could have happened."

The boys stared at him, wide-eyed.

"Tootles has been kidnapped!" Peter declared.

Tink gasped. She was not overly fond of Tootles. He had always tried to catch her and stuff her into his pockets. But—*kidnapped!*

Peter turned to the Lost Boys. "Men, we must rescue Tootles. But it may be dangerous." His eyes twinkled. This was just the sort of adventure he adored. "Only the bravest among you may go with me," he told the boys.

The Lost Boys all wanted to be the bravest. They scrambled to line up behind him.

Tink hesitated. Peter looked back at her. "Aren't you coming, Tink?"

He smiled his reckless smile. It suddenly seemed as if no time had passed since her days with Peter Pan. Swept up in the excitement, Tink forgot all about her search for the pixie dust.

"Of course I'm coming!" she cried.

"Then let's go!" said Peter.

They set off marching through the forest. Tink flew in front. They hadn't gone far, though, when she cried out. Peter stopped short. The boys behind him bumped into each other.

Tink flew down and landed next to a paw print in the mud.

"Tracks! Good job, Tink," Peter said. He knelt beside her to look at the track. "It belongs to a tiger. A big one, from the look of it!"

They found another paw print not far off. Tink, Peter, and the boys followed the tracks. They circled right back to the place where Tootles's tracks ended.

"Oh, no." Suddenly, Tink figured out what had happened. She looked at Peter, her eyes wide.

Peter shook his head sadly. "Poor Tootles has been eaten by a tiger."

The Twins' mouths fell open at the same time. Cubby turned as pale as a fish's belly. All the boys stared at Peter.

"Bow your heads, fellas," Peter instructed. "Poor old Tootles."

With loud sniffles, the Lost Boys lowered their heads. Tink landed on Peter's shoulder and solemnly dimmed her glow.

Peter began a little speech. "We'll never forget Tootles. He was a deadeye with a slingshot."

"Aye," said Cubby, "except when he missed."

Peter went on. "Our friend Tootles was a—"

Rrrrow! Suddenly, they heard a loud growl above them.

"The tiger!" Cubby shrieked. He tried to run, but he tripped over the Twins. All three landed in a heap.

Tink flew up into the tree branches. She began to laugh. "That's no tiger," she said. "It's Tootles!"

The growl came again. Now everyone could tell it wasn't a tiger's roar. It was only Tootles's hungry stomach.

"What are you doing?" Peter asked him.

Tootles looked down from the rope that held him. "Hiding," he replied. "I think I found the best hiding spot."

A few days before, Peter and the Lost Boys had rigged the trap, hoping to catch a tiger. Tootles had stumbled into it by mistake when he was looking for a hiding place.

The boys weren't fooled. "Ha-ha!" Slightly laughed. "Tootles got caught in a tiger trap! Tootles got caught in a tiger trap!"

The other boys took up the cry. "Tootles got caught in a tiger trap!"

Peter flew up to the tree branch. He drew his knife to cut down the rope. As he did, they heard a low, deep growl. All heads swiveled to look at Tootles.

"Wasn't me," Tootles said with a shrug.

"The tiger!" Peter cried, just as a huge beast sprang from the bushes.

Up in the air, Tootles, Peter, and Tink were safe. But the tiger was headed straight for the other Lost Boys.

Without thinking, Tink snatched her sack of fairy dust and turned it upside down over them. "Fly!" she yelled.

They didn't waste a second. The Lost Boys leaped into the air. They just missed being caught in the tiger's claws.

The boys perched in the branches of the surrounding trees. On the ground, the

tiger prowled from trunk to trunk. It twitched its tail and watched them with yellow eyes. But they were out of its reach.

"Can't catch us!" Peter cried at the tiger.

"Nyah, nyah! Can't catch us, tiger!" the other boys echoed. They snatched small fruits from the branches around them and threw them at the big cat.

Annoyed, the tiger finally slunk away. When they were sure it was gone, Peter cut Tootles down.

Slightly puffed up his chest. "We sure showed that tiger!" he declared.

"Nah! If it wasn't for Tink, you'd have been his dinner," Peter told him.

The boys knew it was true. They all turned to look at Tink. "Hooray for

Tinker Bell!" they cheered. Tink's glow turned pink as she blushed.

"She should get an award for bravery," Peter said. He fished around in his pocket. At last he came up with a golden bead the size of a small pea. He threaded a piece of grass through it and hung it around Tink's neck.

"We present this medal to Tinker Bell," he announced, "the best and bravest fairy in Never Land."

Tink's heart swelled. Why had she ever doubted herself? She *was* the best and bravest fairy. And she could still prove it!

"Peter, I have to fly to the Northern Shore," she said. "Can you tell me how far it is?"

"Maybe a half day's flight," Peter replied. "Aw, Tink, don't you want to stick around and play?"

Tink smiled and checked the bag of fairy dust. There was still a little left in the bottom. Enough to take her the rest of the way.

"I'll see you again soon," she told Peter. She waved to the Lost Boys. Then, clutching her medal to her chest, she set out once again for the Northern Shore.

9

By sunset, Tink was weary from flying. But her spirits were high. The wind had grown chilly, and she smelled salt in the air. She felt sure she was close to the Northern Shore.

The sky faded from purple to black. The wind blew harder and grew colder still. It numbed her ears and her hands. Tink thought longingly of the sweater she'd lost in the balloon carrier.

A fat, round moon rose. Back in Pixie Hollow, the Fairy Dance would be starting. Tink imagined her friends gathering in the fairy circle, wearing their finest clothes. She could almost hear the music and the laughter. For a moment, she wished she were there.

But she couldn't give up now.

She went over a crest. Ahead, the ground dropped away into ocean. Waves pounded the rocks on the shore.

The Northern Shore! Tink marveled. *I made it! I made it!*

There could be no doubt about it this time. A glowing silver cloud hovered in the air, just above the water. *It's the cloud of pixie dust,* Tink thought. *Just like in Tor's story.*

Tink beat the air with her wings. Within moments, she was skimming the water. The sound of the surf roared in her ears. Spray from the crashing waves soaked her from head to toe.

But where was the pixie dust?

She hovered, looking this way and that. But the air was misty and damp. She couldn't see far. Her wings began to grow heavy with the salt spray.

Looking down, she saw the water churning against the rocks below. A cold jolt of fear shot through her. If she fell, she would be swallowed by the waves.

Quickly, Tink darted back to shore. She found a dry nook high on the side of a rock. From her spot, she once again looked for the pixie dust. There it was!

Just then, a cloud passed across the
moon. Before Tink's eyes, the pixie dust
changed. It no longer seemed to glow.
And it wasn't really silver; it was . . .

"It's nothing but mist!" Tink's voice
trembled. What she had taken for a
cloud of pixie dust was only spray from
the surf, shining in the moonlight.

That couldn't be right. Surely she was in the wrong spot. There had to be another cloud—the real cloud of pixie dust. There had to!

Tink scoured the coastline with her eyes. But there wasn't a cloud to be seen.

"I came all this way for nothing," she said. "I . . . I failed."

Her legs wobbled. She had to clutch the side of the rock to keep from falling. She had never failed before. Not like this.

Finally, she recovered enough to stand. She ripped the medal Peter had given her from her neck and eyed it scornfully.

"Best," she sneered. "I'm not the best at anything."

She didn't even have the energy to

throw it. Tink opened her hand and let it fall. The bead bounced once off the side of the rock and sank into the ocean.

Tink flew slowly back through the forest toward Pixie Hollow. When she became too tired to go on, she found a large flower and curled up in its petals for a few minutes of rest. But she never slept. Thoughts swirled through her mind like leaves caught in a whirlpool.

After all her effort, she had nothing to give Terence. "He will never want to be my friend now," Tink murmured.

She knew she should fly quickly. She was running low on fairy dust. If it ran out, she might never make it back home. But Tink was in no hurry. What did she have to look forward to?

As Tink pondered this, she heard a crashing sound not far away. It was followed by a thud.

Someone groaned, "Oh, no."

Tink darted around a fig tree and through a tangle of vines. She spotted a big hole in the ground. She crept to the edge and peeped in.

There was Tootles staring back at her.

"Tink!" he cried happily.

"What are you doing down there?" asked Tink.

"Oh." Tootles blushed. "I fell into another trap. We dug this one last week. Peter said we'd catch a bear. Only, it looks like we caught me instead."

"Foolish boy," said Tink.

Tootles nodded. He was used to being called foolish, among other things. "Can you give me some fairy dust to fly out?" he asked.

Tink rolled her eyes. She was really too busy to be looking after this silly boy. *Then again*, she thought with a sigh, *I can't just leave him to the wild animals.*

Tink had only the fairy dust left on her wings. There wasn't enough to help Tootles fly out of the hole. Looking around, she spotted a long, thick vine hanging from a nearby tree. Flapping her wings with all her might, she tugged the end of the vine to the hole. She threw it over the edge.

Tootles grabbed it, and he pulled

himself out. He sat on the edge of the hole, huffing and puffing. "Promise not to tell Peter?" he asked when he'd caught his breath.

Tink had no intention of making such a promise. If Peter had been there, she would have told him at once. As it was, she said nothing.

Tootles took her silence as a yes. "Tinker Bell, you should have an award for bravery," he said. He was trying his best to sound like Peter.

He reached into his pockets. But all he found were a few pebbles. Nothing that could be used as a medal.

Tootles scratched his head. His fingers found a sparrow's feather he'd stuck in his cap. As a rule, Peter did not allow the Lost Boys to wear feathers in their caps, since he wore one himself. But this feather was so tiny and insignificant, it had escaped Peter's notice.

Solemnly, Tootles held out the feather to Tink.

Tink took it. She turned it over in her hands. "It's nothing but a sparrow's feather."

Tootles shrugged. "It's the best thing I've got," he said. "I hope you'll take good care of it." With a wave, he ran off to find the other boys.

Tink stood for a moment, looking at the feather. Then she leaped up and began to fly toward home. She knew what she had to do.

TINK GOT BACK to Pixie Hollow just
before dinnertime. As she neared the
Home Tree kitchen, she smelled chest-
nuts roasting. Her mouth watered. For
two days, she'd had nothing to eat but
berries.

But Tink flew on. There was something she had to do first.

When she reached her workshop,
Tink stopped short in surprise. Terence,

Silvermist, Iridessa, Rosetta, and Fawn were standing outside her door.

Tink hovered uncertainly. She had known she would have to face everyone eventually. But she hadn't expected to do it so soon. *What are they doing here?* she wondered.

They were waiting for her, of course. Terence had been the first to notice she was missing. When she hadn't shown up for the Fairy Dance, he'd gone to Tink's friends. But none of them had seen her. After searching all over Pixie Hollow, they had settled down by her workshop to wait. And to worry.

If Tink was startled to see them, they were even more surprised by the sight of her. They had never seen Tink in

such a state! Her dress was torn. Her arms were scratched. Wisps of hair straggled from her ponytail.

The four fairies rushed over.

"Tink, where have you been?" cried Silvermist.

"We've been so worried!" Rosetta added.

"What happened to you?" asked Fawn.

Normally, Tink didn't like to be fussed over. But she was relieved to get such a warm reception. She let them hug her and brush the twigs from her hair.

As Tink's friends surrounded her, Terence hung back. He wasn't sure she would be glad to see him.

"Tink, what you need is a nice bath,"

said Silvermist. "I'll bring you some hot water."

"You need food," said Iridessa. "How does sunflower soup sound?"

"You'll feel much better in a new dress," said Rosetta. "And I have the perfect thing! I'll be back before you can say 'gorgeous.'"

"You need a nap!" said Fawn. "You can borrow my fluffy feather pillow."

The four fairies flew off. Terence started to follow them.

"Terence, wait," Tink said.

She couldn't give him dust from the Pixie Dust Tree. But she could give him something. And now Tink understood that the gift wasn't important. What mattered was how it was given.

She went to the shelf in her workshop and took down the silver bowl. She placed it in Terence's hands.

"It's a perfect repair," he said. "You can't even tell it was bent. You're the best pots-and-pans fairy around, Tink." He started to hand it back.

But Tink shook her head. "It's for you."

"Why?" Terence asked, startled.

"For being my friend," said Tink.

"Friend? But . . . I've been trying *not* to be your friend. You told me to leave you alone."

Now Tink laughed. Terence thought about how he loved her laugh. It sounded like little silver bells ringing.

"I didn't mean for *good!*" Tink

exclaimed. "I was upset. But I'm not anymore. I've been all over Never Land looking for the perfect present for you." She pointed to the bowl. "It was my first fix ever. I hope you'll take good care of it."

Finally, Terence understood. The bowl might have looked like just a silver bowl, but coming from Tink, it was much more than that. It was an apology.

He smiled. "I know just the place for it."

Then, to Tink's surprise, he flew over and placed it back on her shelf. He didn't need the bowl. Tink's friendship was all he'd ever wanted.

"I think it will be safe here," he told Tink. "And I can come by to visit it.

Now, you look like you need something to eat. Shall we go to dinner?"

Tink laughed. She was messy and covered in dust, but it didn't matter. She took Terence's hand. And together the two friends flew out into the evening.